CHAMPION

JEWISH SPORTS STORIES FOR KIDS

Published by Pitspopany Press
Copyright © 2004

Cover Design by Ben Gasner Studios
Book Design by Tiffen Studios (T.C. Peterseil)

Pitspopany Press titles may be purchased for fundraising programs
by schools and organizations by contacting:

Marketing Director, Pitspopany Press
40 East 78th Street, Suite 16D
New York, New York 10021
Tel: (800) 232-2931
Fax: (212) 472-6253
Email: pitspop@netvision.net.il

ISBN: 1-930143-66-4 Cloth
ISBN: 1-930143-67-2 Paper

Printed in Israel

TABLE OF CONTENTS

THE QUEEN OF SLOW MOTION   5
BY JUDY LABENSOHN

THE KILLER FAN   35
BY YAACOV PETERSEIL

THE SEVENTH INNING BOMB   69
BY AVRAHAM BERGER

SH'MA!   95
BY ELIOT FINTUSHEL

THE ALL-STAR SUPER KLUTZ   123
BY TONI LYNN DOVE

GREAT SAVE!   149
BY DEBBIE SPRING

BASEBALL BLUES   169
BY TOVAH S. YAVIN

THE DOOTCH   203
BY CRAIG LEWIS

OTHER BOOKS IN THIS SERIES:

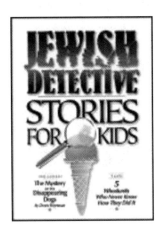

THE QUEEN OF SLOW MOTION

BY JUDY LABENSOHN

Judy Labensohn

I first came to Israel in 1966 and fell in love with the country. In 1967, after I graduated from the University of Michigan, I moved to Jerusalem. In those days, the things I missed most about the USA were a good paper napkin, an English library, and the Cleveland Indians.

I love to write today as much as I did in third grade. But now I am even luckier, because I help others who want to write develop their writing skills. You can learn more about this at www.writeinisrael.com.

Can you believe I have three children, all born in Israel, who have never played baseball?

But I still love them.

THE QUEEN OF SLOW MOTION

On Shabbat afternoons, Barbara Greenfield loved nothing more than to sprawl on her living room couch and read. One Shabbat in June, when she was reading *The Jerusalem Post*, she saw an ad that made her jump. Such a jump was unusual for a fifty-seven year old woman who, over a lifetime, had perfected the art of sitting and sprawling.

```
Women's Softball Team Needs You.
No  Experience  Necessary.
Call The Chariots, 08-6726172
NS. (Not on Shabbat)
```

The Chariots? Once in an upright position, Barbara imagined standing behind a chariot pulled by two graceful horses, galloping around a baseball diamond to home plate. She heard rowdy crowds in a large amphitheater cheer for her, as they did during the famous chariot race in *Ben Hur*, her favorite movie. This was perfect for a woman who wouldn't even run for a bus.

Barbara looked at her watch. 5:17 P.M. Only three hours left before she could call.

Slowness was the reason Barbara had chosen to live in Jerusalem. She loved the lingering pace of

the city's Shabbatot. Everyone slowed down to a shuffle, even the joggers. Businesses and buses stopped altogether. Jerusalem became a slow-motion city; a city in tune with Barbara's pace.

Although the nickname "Slowpoke" had stuck with her from second grade, in her heart Barbara never stopped wondering if, perhaps, there was a runner, a fast runner, buried inside her, aching to be set free.

This ad might be my ticket to change, she thought, as she checked her watch again.

Forty-seven years ago, when she was ten, Barbara Greenfield had spent her Saturday afternoons watching Al Rosen play third base at the Cleveland Stadium. During the week she collected photographs of Al and her favorite teammates on the Cleveland Indians—outfielders Rocky Colavito and Larry Doby. She sat and pasted the pictures into her scrapbook. This was her *hana'ah* (enjoyment): Rocky, Larry and Al smiling at her, just at her, from the gray pages of her scrapbook.

Al was her favorite Indian because he was Jewish, like her. She felt proud that someone who went to her Temple on Yom Kippur, who probably lit candles on Hanukkah and hid the *afikoman* at the Seder, could also run fast and become a Cleveland Indian.

Barbara sprawled back down on her couch and tried to read, but snoozed instead, the newspaper over her face. When she awoke, she checked her

8
CHAMPION

watch, 7:17 P.M. One hour to go. Yes, she would call The Chariots, at least to get information. She sat up and thought about the Indians. Going to games with a friend was always fun. While seated in the stands behind first base, she watched the young men roam the stairs, yelling in baseball English, "Be-a he-a, be-a he-a." After a few games, she learned that, in regular English, this meant "Beer Here." Between innings, she and her friend would go to the food stands and buy Hebrew National hot dogs. She loved the steaming, mushy buns, made even mushier with Cleveland's famous Stadium Mustard.

For a slow person like Barbara, the stands were an excellent place. There she felt part of something larger and more exciting than her own, slow, fifth grade self. She loved the roar of the fans when Al Rosen hit a homer. She imagined all his home runs flying over the fence and falling into Lake Erie, where they turned into gefilte fish. Even today, forty-seven years later, the idea made her laugh.

Sitting in the stands gave her time for imagining. Sometimes, Barbara even imagined herself on the diamond. Though the fish fantasy could occupy her for twenty minutes, the image of her actually playing baseball on any field never lasted more than twenty seconds. It was ridiculous, after all. In fifth

9

CHAMPION

grade, Barbara Greenfield was the slowest runner in Fairfield Elementary, probably in the whole State of Ohio.

"It's genetic," she would tell Mrs. Van Meter, the school coach, each year in September during the first day of gym. "My grandmother never ran fast. My Mom strolls. The only thing that runs fast in our family is *slowness*."

"But what's stopping *you*, Barbara?" Mrs. Van Meter asked every year, putting a kind hand on her shoulder.

"I don't know," Barbara replied year after year. "Even when I sit on the swings in the playground, I keep one foot scraping the ground to slow down. Fast scares me."

Again Barbara looked at her watch, 7:37 P.M. She tried reading the sports section, but she couldn't concentrate. Thinking of Fairfield Elementary reminded her of how much she hated gym, especially standing against the wall when team leaders chose kids for Capture the Flag and Red Rover. She got used to being the last person chosen, but still, it hurt.

I won't call The Chariots, she decided. *Maybe I'll just sit and read a book about baseball. Why try out for a team sport and get hurt again?*

She re-read the ad. The words *"No Experience Necessary"* made her rethink her decision. Barbara looked at her watch, 7:47 P.M. *Well, yes, maybe I will call.*

For the last half-hour of Shabbat, Barbara weighed the pros and cons of calling The Chariots.

Since she had always been a lousy runner, Barbara had perfected the art of sitting. Over the years, she sat in libraries, classes, workshops, and lectures. She never went on marches, but was always available for sit-ins, be they for civil rights or against the Vietnam War. Barbara acquired several degrees by sitting. By the time she was twenty-five, she had a Ph.D in psychology, a profession that guaranteed her many years of sitting in one place. Her patients, always running in and out, were those on the playing field of life, while she continued to watch from her chair, cheering.

Often, Barbara had to remind herself that she was no longer ten and living in Cleveland, but rather fifty-seven and a citizen of Jerusalem, Israel. True, she had changed countries. Going to Israel had been her attempt to get on the playing field of Jewish history, rather than on the sidelines in the Diaspora. But even in Israel, even in a town full of walkable hills, Barbara closed herself up in an office, sat on a chair, listened to clients and read. Even though she looked grown-up, inside, she was still the ten-year-old slowpoke, scared to play ball, frightened to run. Yet, she still dreamed of taking the field.

Barbara looked at the ad again:

Women's Softball Team Needs You!

"Me?" she asked the ad.

At 8:17 P.M. she sauntered to the phone and plopped down in the chair next to it. While her fingers dialed the number, her brain hoped nobody would answer.

"*Shavua tov,*" (good week) came a man's voice. He sounded energetic, well-rested and happy.

"Shavua tov," Barbara replied. "I...ah...saw your...ah...ad and ah...." Barbara felt her pulse race as her words almost came to a halt.

"Oh, you want to play softball? Great. You can join The Chariots. I'm Aryeh, their coach. Great team. Wonderful group of women. Are you free on Tuesday evening at 6:15?"

Barbara had hardly formed a sentence and this man, Aryeh, was already putting her on the team.

"I...ah...don't run very fast." There, she said it, put it right up front, handing it to him like a calling card.

"6:15, 6:20. What did you say your name is?"

"Barbara," she said, then swallowed slowly. "Barbara Greenfield. But I've never...never played ...softball...or...."

"Do you know where Gezer is? That's where we play all our games. Ten minutes beyond Latrun. Of course, that's if you're coming from Jerusalem. If you're coming from Tel Aviv, it's five minutes past Ramle. Can you get there on Tuesday at sixish?"

"I'm fifty-seven," Barbara blurted.

"We practice for forty-five minutes, give or take, and we start playing at seven."

Was he deaf, Barbara wondered, or just hard up for players? Couldn't he understand that she was old and that "I don't run very fast" was an understatement?

"Al Rosen."

"What?" Aryeh asked, startled. Barbara realized she had finally broken through to him.

"I used to love Al Rosen. I rooted for the Indians...My computer mouse pad has the insignia of the Cleveland Indians."

"Great. That's just great. So now you'll root for yourself and The Chariots. What did you say your name is?"

"Barbara. Barbara Greenfield."

"Listen Barbara, on Tuesday you'll have to play as Batsheva. She's one of our best players, but she went back to New York for the summer. The insurance policy is in her name. I can't change the policy, so I hope you don't mind if we call you Batsheva for the season."

The season? Barbara was still struggling with the idea of playing and here was this Aryeh, this male coach of a women's softball team called The Chariots, putting her in the lineup for the season.

She considered hanging up, but then a voice

13

CHAMPION

from her past shouted: *v'im lo achshav ey matai?* (If not now—when?)

"You want me to play more than once?" Her tone gained confidence. "You haven't even seen me move."

Barbara looked at the wrinkles on her hands. She was probably old enough to be Aryeh's mother.

"No problem," Aryeh soothed. "Come to Gezer on Tuesday. They have great lighting out there and it's a beautiful field. We're playing the Black Hebrews from Dimona."

While Aryeh caught his breath, Barbara thought of Larry Doby, the first African-American player in the American League, the all-star center fielder for the Indians from 1949 to 1955. On Tuesday, if she indeed went to Gezer, she would play against a whole team of female Larry Doby's. No doubt they would be fast runners and hard hitters. She shuddered.

As if reading her mind, Aryeh said, "Don't worry, don't worry. It's softball, not baseball. Distances are shorter. The ball is bigger. We just get out there on the field and do it for fun."

Barbara looked at her hands again and noticed her dark, age spots. She wondered if her hands would be able to catch a ball. Then she hummed, *v'im lo achshav ey matai.*

"OK," Barbara muttered. "OK, I'll come." How could she let down The Chariots? They were obviously so needy, they took the first caller. She could be ninety and Aryeh would have taken her. "By the

way, I don't have a mitt. And, what should I wear?"

"Wear a black skirt or black slacks and a gray T-shirt. That's The Chariots' uniform. I bring all the equipment."

Skirt? How could anyone play baseball in a skirt, Barbara wondered. Then she realized that the team was probably made up of at least some Orthodox women who didn't wear slacks.

"*Shalom and l'hitra'ot,*" (good-bye) Aryeh said. "See you on Tuesday."

"Shavua tov," replied Barbara.

This time her words were more like an expression of hope than a greeting.

After she hung up, Barbara stood and stretched her arms towards the ceiling. Then she pinched her right arm, her pitching arm, to see if she was fully conscious. She felt strangely excited, as if she had just made a date with Al Rosen himself.

On Tuesday, Barbara drove west out of Jerusalem down the pine-covered hills towards Tel Aviv. Ten minutes after Latrun, she arrived at Kibbutz Gezer in the Judean lowlands. She followed the kibbutz signs to the playing field. When she got out of her car, she saw a real ballpark covered with well-

kept grass, a diamond, a pitcher's mound, and a professional-looking backstop. There were no dugouts, but each team had a wooden bench behind a wire fence. Tall poles near the first and third baselines held spotlights. There was even a stand that sold popsicles and kosher *(glatt)* hotdogs.

The baseball field was at the foot of an archaeological *tel* (mound.) Tel Gezer was the site of the city of Gezer, which was more than five thousand years old. On Sunday and Monday, Barbara had read up on Gezer, because the team's name did not sit right with her. She thought it might be connected to Gezer, but wasn't sure. Once she learned a little of Gezer's history, though, The Chariots made perfect sense.

King Solomon had gained possession of Gezer when he married an Egyptian princess. The princess and her father, the Pharaoh, gave the city to King Solomon as a wedding present. Solomon fortified the town and used it to store his vast wealth of olive oil and wheat. He also built stables in Gezer for the horses that pulled his many chariots. In fact, King Solomon was the first leader who used chariots as military weapons. As soon as Barbara read this, she knew why the team was called The Chariots.

Now the famous archaeological site, with its fallen boulders that once served as the city's walls and stone gates, provided a backdrop for a softball game between the Black Hebrews of Dimona and The Chariots. When Barbara looked up at Tel Gezer,

a sense of pride made her stand taller than her five foot one inch. She pushed back her shoulders and walked towards her team's bench, her thoughts lost in a mish-mash of kings, chariots, Indians, and gefilte fish.

Barbara was taken aback when she saw the professional outfits of the Black Hebrews from Dimona. Each player wore a shiny red shirt and matching colored slacks. Printed on the back of each shirt was the player's number. The Black Hebrews looked like a real team. They even brought a cheering section of fifteen men and nine kids.

Her own team looked wimpy, in comparison. There were five women in long black skirts, gray head coverings, and gray T-shirts that covered their elbows. These were Orthodox Jews from the United States who had settled in Beit Shemesh, a town between Jerusalem and Gezer. In addition, there were three high school girls from Kibbutz Gezer who wore black Bermuda shorts and gray tank tops. White head-bands caught the sweat dripping from their foreheads. Each girl had her own mitt that looked well-used. The girls told Barbara that their parents had come to Israel from the United States and passed on their love of baseball and softball to them. At the end of the summer, all three girls would be joining the Israeli army.

17
CHAMPION

Barbara did a quick calculation. She was old enough to be everyone's mother and even the youngest girls' grandmother.

"You must be Batsheva," a familiar voice said in a singsong. Barbara turned around and saw a man who definitely needed to jog. His bulging stomach made it difficult to carry the bats and mitts, so he dragged them on the ground behind him in a laundry bag. He wore a gray T-shirt that barely covered his belly. It had three galloping horses on it.

"Couldn't find one with a chariot," he joked, dropping the bag. Aryeh's bearded face was as round as his stomach. When he smiled, which was after every sentence, his red cheeks rolled into his eyes. He was the only man on the Chariots' bench, other than the pitcher's five-year-old son.

"Welcome. Thanks for coming." Then Aryeh turned to all the women who were discussing their kids, husbands, boyfriends, work, diets, and army service. "Hey guys. This is Batsheva." The women looked at her, smiled, and thanked her for coming.

Then Aryeh started clapping his hands, as if to bring the group's focus back to the game. "OK team. Let's get out there and run around the field a few times to warm up." Exhausted, he sat down on the bench.

That's the job for me, Barbara thought, watching Aryeh take a long drink from a bottle of water.

Barbara slowly walked to home plate. Then she turned to Aryeh and yelled, "Do you want us to run

18

CHAMPION

around the bases or the whole field?"

"The whole field," he shouted.

Barbara hadn't run since sixth grade, forty-five years earlier. In junior high and high school, she had chosen fencing for gym. She didn't know if she *could* run around the whole field.

I should have consulted Dr. Regel, she thought, as she ran towards first base. *What if I faint? What if I have a heart attack?*

After about fifteen seconds, Barbara slowed down to an earnest walk, then her traditional shuffle.

The field seemed enormous. Barbara never realized how much distance there was from the diamond to the outfield. When she reached the fence that separated the playing field from Tel Gezer, she turned left and began mumbling. *Why did I answer that ad? Why did I leave my slow city? How will I make it through the game? Why aren't I doing what I do best in the evenings—sitting and reading or watching TV?*

By the time Barbara reached the third base line, she broke into a heavy sweat. Even though a Mediterranean breeze was cooling the field, she felt run down. Her heart skipped beats. She thought she would faint. She couldn't play softball. No, not today. Not ever. She had missed her chance to join a

team and run on a field...by about forty-five years.

Nonetheless, Barbara Greenfield didn't give up. She dragged her sweaty body all the way to home plate and beyond. When she reached The Chariots' bench, she collapsed

"Here, have some water." A woman in a long black skirt handed her a canteen. "I'm Chana."

"Uh," Barbara sat up, took the canteen, and gulped. She thought she might throw up. "I don't think I can...do this...I can't...run...the risk...." She gave back the canteen and leaned over. Her head plopped into her hands. Breathe deeply, she told herself.

Chana put a hand on Barbara's head. "What risk?"

"Dying," Barbara replied.

"You'll be fine," Chana said. "You probably haven't run in a long time."

"Yeah," Barbara said softly. "Forever is a pretty long time...Is there a team doctor?"

"No. Does something hurt?"

"I don't know...I can't feel anything yet."

Barbara sensed eyes staring at her from the end of the bench. When her breathing returned to normal, she lifted her head, turned, and saw a girl of about ten sitting and fidgeting with her hair.

"That's my daughter, Ma'ayan," Chana said

"Hi," Barbara offered, giving her a hi-five.

Ma'ayan returned a soft "Hi," while staring at the ground.

"Do you play softball?" Barbara asked, her voice quiet and low.

"I can't," Ma'ayan replied, almost in a whisper.

"Why not?"

After a few moments of awkward silence, Chana broke in. "She caught her foot in a lawn mower when she was five, so she can't run."

"So what?" Barbara said, moving her eyes from mother to daughter. "I can't run either, and I've never even been near a lawn mower. Did you see me, Ma'ayan?"

"Mmmm," Ma'ayan said. She held back a smile.

"Ma'ayan, you're probably a good watcher, aren't you?" Barbara said. Ma'ayan did not respond. Barbara was starting to feel better. "And I bet your pasting skills are top-notch." Barbara could tell Ma'ayan was listening because she stopped fidgeting with her hair. "I was a good watcher too, Ma'ayan." Barbara paused and wiped the sweat from her forehead with her hand. "Until today."

Ma'ayan laughed.

"OK, so I can't run fast, so what? I may look dead, but I'm not dead yet, am I?" Barbara could feel her voice growing stronger.

Ma'ayan said, "No."

"You can sit, watch, and wait, Ma'ayan. Maybe one day when your hair is gray like mine, you'll de-

21

cide to try to run." Barbara put her fingers through her gray bangs. "That day may be in 2048." Barbara stared at Ma'ayan for a moment. "Or it could be tomorrow."

Ma'ayan's eyes widened.

Meanwhile, all the women on the team were trying on mitts. It was time to go out to the field to practice throwing and catching.

"Do you want a piece of banana cake?" Chana asked Barbara. "I made it for Shabbat, but there was some left over."

Barbara wondered if Al Rosen ate his mother's leftover Shabbat cakes before a game.

"No thanks, Chana," Barbara said. "I think right now is a good time for me to begin my softball diet. Cake will slow me down to a crawl."

"I understand," Chana said, as she handed Barbara a mitt.

"Which hand do I put it on?" As soon as the words were out of her mouth, Barbara felt embarrassed. She heard Ma'ayan laugh.

"It's for a righty, so put it on your left hand."

"Just checking," Barbara said, meekly. She put the mitt on her left hand. Suddenly, she felt stronger, the way a charioteer might have felt when he put the helmet on his head and took the reigns.

"Let's throw a few to each other," Chana said, pushing her right fist into her glove. The movement reminded Barbara of Rocky, Larry, and Al. She mimicked Chana.

22

They strolled out to center field, where the smell of freshly cut grass almost overwhelmed Barbara. The setting sun had turned the sky a glazed pink. Standing there, Barbara thought the Gezer baseball field was the most beautiful site in Israel, more beautiful than Ein Gedi, more exciting than Caesarea. She was glad she had finally discovered it, after so many years of sitting.

Chana threw the ball to Barbara, who watched it fall about four feet to her right. She walked over to pick it up and threw it back to Chana. Chana's next ball fell on the ground about two feet to Barbara's left. Barbara watched it hit the grass.

"You're supposed to run and catch the ball, Batsheva," Chana yelled at her. "Don't wait until it comes to you. Not all the balls will come directly to you."

Chana's suggestion was remarkable in its simplicity. *Go out to meet the ball. Don't just stand in one place and wait for the ball to come to you.* Barbara knew instantly that that was how she had lived her life. She had stood still, even though she had changed countries. She waited for something to happen, rather than going out to make it happen. For Chana's next throw, Barbara would run and meet the ball. Even if she didn't catch it, which she didn't,

23

CHAMPION

at least she was moving in the right direction.

"OK. That's it," came Aryeh's voice from the bench. "Let's run back home."

This time, Barbara jogged all the way back to the bench.

When everyone was back on the bench, Aryeh assigned positions.

"Remember," he pointed to Barbara and winked, "this is Batsheva." Then he turned to her and said, "Batsheva, you'll play right field."

Barbara waved good-bye to Ma'ayan, who hadn't moved from the edge of the bench. "Wish me luck," she begged. Ma'ayan lifted her chin, a sign Barbara interpreted as support. She walked out to the field slowly and positioned herself.

"Let's move to the left a little, Batsheva," Aryeh yelled from the bench. Barbara followed his directions. Then she hunkered down, punched her mitt, and shifted her weight from side to side. Years of watching baseball had paid off. She knew how outfielders looked and moved, and now she could at least act like a real player.

"Batter up," yelled the umpire. Barbara felt her body tense from a surge of adrenaline. Her lips went dry. She hadn't felt this excited since the first day she had landed in Israel.

A player from the Black Hebrews of Dimona stepped up to the plate. Barbara put on a mean, tough expression, so the batter would, hopefully, be afraid to hit the ball in her direction. While swaying

from side to side, she prayed to the God of Abraham, Isaac, and Jacob, Sarah, Rebecca, Leah, and Rachel: *Dear God, please let all the balls go to center or left field.*

During the first inning, God answered her prayers.

Even though she did nothing but sway and look tough, Barbara felt like part of the action, part of the team. Her concentration had not wavered for a second. She always kept her eye on the ball. She especially liked the other team's chant. Whenever a Black Hebrew batter came to the plate, all fifteen men and nine children sang:

> *Quitters never win.*
> *And winners never quit.*
> *Step up to the plate.*
> *And get yourself a hit.*

They chanted this over and over again, clapping their hands, snapping their fingers, and moving their whole bodies as if they were at a revival meeting. Barbara liked the rhythm and swayed to the beat every time the cheering section from Dimona sang. She hoped her enthusiasm for the opposing team's cheer would not undermine her allegiance to The Chariots. She wished her team had some jive or rap cheer, some catchy tune she could repeat to

herself like a mantra. But every time she glanced at The Chariots' bench, all she saw was the pitcher's five-year-old son eating pretzels and Ma'ayan playing with her hair.

The Black Hebrews made four runs during the first inning. Now The Chariots were up to bat. When it was Barbara's turn to bat, she put on a blue helmet and took a few practice swings with a blue aluminum bat. She had never seen an aluminum bat. The Indians only used wooden bats.

"Go for it, Batsheva," her teammates shouted as she approached the plate. Being called a different name helped her forget her fear. Barbara couldn't hit to save her life, but Batsheva would be one of the best hitters on the team. Standing at home plate, she touched it several times with the bat. Then she got into position, knees bent, shoulders straight, just like Rocky, Larry, and Al. She looked straight into the pitcher's eyes.

"Show'em your stuff, Batsheva," her teammates called.

Batsheva swallowed, put on a tough face, and ignored her irregular heartbeat.

"Show'em what ya got, Batsheva," Chana yelled.

Barbara had thought up a brilliant plan that Batsheva would execute. She frowned and looked mean. Barbara wanted the pitcher to be scared of Batsheva. Then the nervous, psyched-out pitcher would throw four wild balls and walk the batter. Barbara could stroll to first base, at her own pace.

Unfortunately, this pitcher knew how to pitch. She wasn't scared of anyone, not Batsheva and certainly not Barbara. Her first two throws went right over the plate. Barbara froze as the umpire shouted, "Strike" each time. On the third pitch, Barbara swung the bat. It made a clinking sound, like a coin falling on cement. After a second, Barbara realized that the sound meant she had hit the ball.

"Run, Batsheva, run!" The Chariots cried from the bench.

Barbara dropped the bat and ran as fast as she could. Though her heart raced, her legs moved in a spirited waddle. She could see the softball going straight to first base, along the same line she was following. She knew it would get there before her, so she slowed down to a shuffle.

"Keep running, Batsheva! Keep running!" her teammates yelled. "Open 'er up!" one of them called.

Meanwhile, the woman playing first base ran to pick up the ball, but it rolled through her legs. When Barbara saw this, she plunged towards the base.

"Safe," an umpire yelled.

Barbara turned to her teammates. Her face wasn't wide enough to contain her smile.

"Way to go, Batsheva! Way to go!" they shouted. Even Ma'ayan smiled.

The fact that The Chariots lost 21 to 6 did not, in any way, ruin the fun Barbara Greenfield had that night. Five times she had gone up to bat; five times she had hit the ball; five times she had made it to first base. Three times she was even safe.

During the week that followed, when she recalled the glorious clink of the bat hitting the ball, she was moved to tears. The sound, though hollow and high, had as much power as the sound of a shofar on Rosh Hashana. Both sounds urged her to take stock of who she was, of what she could accomplish, if she only dared.

Barbara couldn't wait until the next game. All week she suffered from what her grandmother called *shpilkes* (needles). For the first time in her life, she couldn't sit still. She even wondered if sitting had run its course. All she could think about was the next game.

On Tuesday, she arrived fifteen minutes early. She started running around the whole field at her Barbara pace, even before Aryeh arrived. This time, she only had to rest for five minutes after circling the field and she was fairly confident she wouldn't die.

The Chariots were playing The Walnuts, a hard-hitting team from Tel Aviv. Their pitcher had won a college scholarship somewhere in Connecticut for playing softball. They practiced twice a week, unlike The Chariots, who never practiced. Barbara was scared, scared that she wouldn't be able to connect

with the ball and scared that she'd mess up if a hit came to her in right field.

We're here for the fun, we're here for the fun, she kept telling herself.

The Walnuts were up to bat first. Indeed, their players were fabulous hitters, but again Barbara prayed and again, God answered her prayer. All the hits either went to the left fielder or to the shortstop. The Walnuts' pitcher struck out the first three Chariot batters. She threw so fast Barbara could hardly keep her eye on the ball. Barbara went to bat during the second inning. There were two outs. Barbara swung. She heard the clink. She watched the ball whiz between the pitcher and first base.

"Run, Batsheva, run!" The Chariots yelled.

Barbara ran her slow run and was safe on first. Then Chana came to bat. She hit the second pitch to the shortstop. Barbara glanced behind her at Ma'ayan who was beaming with pride. Suddenly, everyone started shouting, "Run, Batsheva, run!" Barbara began to move, picking up speed like a locomotive leaving the station. When she stopped, she found herself on second base.

Barbara had never been to second base before. She smiled hello at the Walnut player standing next to her, as if she, Barbara, was a visitor expecting

29
CHAMPION

coffee and cookies. There were two outs, a Chariot on first and second. Tirza, one of the girls going into the Israeli army at the end of the summer, was up at bat.

"Tir-za! Tir-za!" The Chariots screamed.

Tirza waited for the right pitch and when it came she hit the ball low and hard to center field. Again Barbara heard "Run, Batsheva, run!" so she started to move. The distance between second and third seemed longer than that between first and second, but she kept moving until she touched the base. The night lights came on, blinding everyone for a moment. She couldn't believe it. Never in her wildest fantasies had she believed that one day she would stand on third base as a runner, as a member of a team that needed her, someone who had run from first to second to third. She waved to The Chariots on the bench and made the V-for-victory sign with both hands. Her teammates laughed. Ma'ayan stood up and glued her face to the fence.

Barbara turned around to look at Tel Gezer. It stood encircled by darkness and silence. She imagined King Solomon watching the softball game from the bleachers, sitting with his Egyptian princess, sipping wine. She imagined Larry Doby, Rocky Colavito, and Al Rosen sitting next to them, cheering her on and eating kosher hot dogs. Then she saw Mrs. Van Meter pushing her way in, looking for a seat. They had all come to watch her play and suddenly Barbara understood that they were all on her side. They

30

CHAMPION

wanted her to play, no matter how she ran.

She waved to them and they waved back. Then she turned to the game. Ofra was swinging the bat at home plate.

"Come on, Ofra, bring me home!" The voice was Barbara's, sung almost as a prayer.

Ofra, wearing a long black skirt, a scarf on her head and black-rimmed glasses, swung twice and missed. Two outs, two strikes, bases loaded. On the next pitch, Ofra slammed a solid hit out to left center field. Barbara stood and watched it slip by the woman playing second base and fall out of the center fielder's glove, while all the time she heard yelling and screaming. The rowdy calls pushed her back to the chariot race in Ben Hur, but when she heard the name, "Batsheva!" she realized that now, she was the chariot.

She faced home plate and leapt into the air. She skipped and pranced over the flat Gezer field like the gazelles in King Solomon's *Song of Songs*. But her leaps were different. They looked like the graceful, slow-motion strides in films, when directors wanted to show the beauty of movement. This was Barbara's normal speed—slow motion—but now she accepted it for what it was. Not only did she accept it, she celebrated it, she wallowed in it,

31

CHAMPION

waving her arms in the air, as if somewhere between third base and home plate, she might take off and fly. Her movement no more resembled a run than a softball resembles a matzo ball, but it did its work. It helped her leap over centuries and millennia, back to 955 BCE when King Solomon reigned in Gezer, and forward to 1955 CE when the Indians played in the Stadium. The way she moved helped her straddle over continents and oceans, from Gezer to Cleveland and back to Jerusalem. Imaginary horses pulled her along, making her go forward, forward. In slow motion she ran into her fears and flew through them and in slow motion she broke through all those self-effacing thoughts that had kept her a sitter rather than a mover, a watcher rather than a doer.

Home plate was two steps away, but she felt like she hadn't even touched ground since leaving third base. In the background, she heard the *Ben Hur* noises, but she couldn't understand what her Chariots were shouting, so lost was she in the magnificence of her own, slow pace. All she knew was that she had a goal, a direction, and that Aryeh and the good women on her team who accepted her and let her play according to her own ability, just for the fun of it, were clapping. As her left foot touched home plate, her arms flew into the air. She turned in a circle, around and around, like she had seen Nadia Comaneci do, the Romanian champion gymnast, when she won Olympic gold medals in 1976. A huge grin covered her face. She was victorious. She had

32

CHAMPION

touched all the bases and reached home plate. Now she knew for sure. There was no fast runner buried inside her. There was only Barbara, waiting to celebrate herself. Turning round and round on home plate, she accepted the cheers. Slow was beautiful. Slow was fine. And she was its Queen.

That the pitcher had tagged her out before she touched home plate didn't matter to her, and it didn't matter to The Chariots either. It was just a game. And she had won the toughest and longest battle of all. Her teammates understood this victory.

"Way to go, Batsheva!" they cried, "Way to go!"

When she reached the bench, they patted her helmet, her shoulders, back, and arms, just like the team did to Rocky, Larry, and Al when they hit homers. Barbara felt so uplifted by circling the diamond at her own pace that words from the Talmud ran out of her mouth: *Im ain ani li, mi li?* (If I don't root for myself, who will root for me?) When The Chariots joined in the refrain, the team discovered its chant: *V'im ani rok l'atzmi, mah ani?* (And if I'm only out for myself, then what kind of person am I?).

Ma'ayan came over to stand in Barbara/Batsheva's presence, to absorb some of the royal rays of the Queen of Slow Motion. Suddenly, she gave Barbara a hug. Barbara took off her helmet and

·CHAMPION·

placed it, like a crown, on Ma'ayan's head. All The Chariots joined hands and formed a circle around Barbara/Batsheva and Ma'ayan. They clapped and sang, *v'im lo achshav, ey matai, v'im lo achshav, ey matai, v'im lo achshav, ey matai, ey matai.* (And if not now, when?).

Meanwhile, Aryeh, sitting on the bench, said, "Let's pack up."

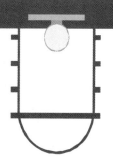

THE KILLER FAN

BY Yaacov Peterseil

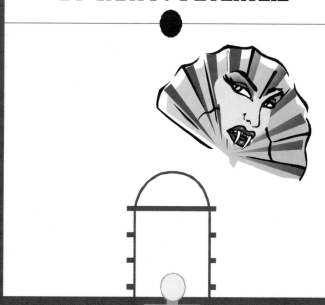

35

CHAMPION

Yaacov Peterseil

I've always admired those people you see at a game, fearlessly shouting for a team or a player. It takes a certain amount of guts to get up and shout like that; guts I sadly lack.

I remember, as a kid, just once shouting for my team. I yelled louder and stronger than anyone else. I felt great. Only thing was, I was sitting on the opposing side's bench and found myself face-to-face with lots of people shouting at me. That kind of experience can really stifle a person.

So after I grew up a bit, I decided that if I wasn't going to yell at games, at least I should marry someone who would.

There are some people who say that the heroine of this story is based on my lovely wife. I want everyone to know that that's absolutely not true.

We only have nine kids.

THE KILLER FAN

You've got to admire my Mom. Not because she's married to my father (that's another story), and not because she has eleven kids (that's an even bigger story), but because she somehow manages, during any 24 hour period, to worry about each one of us and—here's the kicker—she's always there when we need her.

Think about it. Eleven kids.

Ten pregnancies (the first were twins), no help (except on Fridays), round-the-clock carpools; thirty-three meals a day—almost none served at the same time; two hungry washing machines and two creaking dryers to feed, non-stop; story hour at night every night from 8:00; ballet lessons, karate lessons, flute lessons, oboe lessons, piano lessons, drum lessons, tennis lessons, hockey practice at *least* once a week; driving to the doctor almost daily; scheduling school tutors, play dates, sleepovers, and the always in demand "time with Mom".

Oh, did I mention basketball practice at least twice a week? And attending basketball games during the season?

Mom doesn't like us to call her "Super Mom" but that's how all of us feel about her. She's always there for us. Always.

Like when Sheila, one of my younger sisters

went to the movies with some friends and found out that the movie they wanted to see was rated R (for excessive violence). She calls Mom, crying about how they have nothing to do and no place to go now that they can't get into the movie theater without a parent. What does Mom do? You guessed it, she drops everything (and everyone, including my six-month-old sister, Shira), calls me to baby-sit, and goes to the movies with six thirteen-year-olds.

And sits through a movie she hates.

Or when Rivki, one of my other younger sisters decides to bake a cake for the class party. She gets all the ingredients, but doesn't quite know how to go about putting them together (she's seven). Mom's busy doing homework with Sandy (she's eleven), one of my other younger sisters, so she calls yours truly to take over the studying. What do I remember about The Civil War? How am I supposed to help Sandy *Recreate the Battle of Gettysburg, emphasizing the strategy each side used to try and win?*

Meanwhile, Mom's busy baking this humongous cake. You'd think that would make Rivki happy. You'd think. But no, she wants the name of each of the twenty-two girls in her class written with frosting on the cake "so they can eat their names." Of course Mom does it. And when they run out of frosting who has to run to the grocery store for more?

I could go on but as I said earlier, the kids are another story, a very long story.

My point is that Mom is always ready to get in

there and help. That's good.

And sometimes, not so good.

Like at basketball games.

I play center for my high school team, the Yeshiva Hillel Oreos. Don't ask. We got the name Oreos when Oreos became Kosher. The coach was always telling us that when he was a kid he wasn't all that kosher and he loved Oreos because they were crunchy on the outside and creamy on the inside. He told us that there was a lot to learn about eating an Oreo cookie. Things like how to get your tongue in-between the two pieces of cookie and sort of swipe the creamy filling, like a teaser. Then there was the hard, but important, job of gently lifting one of the cookie halves so that almost none of the creamy inside would cling to it. Then you had to eat the cookie. Slowly. Always looking down at the creamy part. And finally, when you had swallowed the cookie part (only the top cookie part, of course) then you sort of puckered up and gave the cream a big kiss, sucking it in. The second cookie part he called a "chaser", whatever that means.

I'm only telling you all this so you'll understand what a nut our coach is, and what a fanatic about Oreo cookies. So, when Oreos became kosher (I'm still not clear when that happened), he immediately

39

CHAMPION

asked the school to change our name from the Ye-shiva Hillel Mavens to the Yeshiva Hillel Oreos. Rabbi Oberon said yes because he had no idea what Oreos were. I know that because he always refers to our team as the Yeshiva Hillel Orioles, like the name of the baseball team.

Anyway, the coach says that the most impor-tant lesson to learn from Oreo cookies is that you have to be hard on the outside but smooth as cream on the inside. That's how a team has to play. Hard but smooth.

I'm not sure any of us really understand what the coach means, but he constantly drills his "hard but smooth" theory into us. We even have a special Oreo handshake. When any of the team members meet in the hallways at school we always bang el-bows (hard) and then sort of shimmy down the other guy's hand with our forearm, palm, and fingers (smooth). I used to think it was dumb, but I sort of got used to it.

So, as I was saying, my Mom gets carried away sometimes. She means well. Real well. But you know how it is. Sometimes you get so caught up with mean-ing well things turn out well...done (as in ruined).

Like the semifinal game against Yeshiva Toras Banim (YTB).

We've been having an ongoing competition with those guys since before I came to this school. Usu-ally one of us ends up in the finals and, on rare occa-sions, we go head-to-head in the Yeshiva League Finals.

The way the league is set up, your team gets to play every team in the league at least once. There are twelve teams in the League. The teams with the most wins after the first round go on to the second round and play each other. Then there's a third round. After the third round there are the quarters, the semis, and finally, the finals.

We played YTB last week. Their team name is M&Ms (do you have to ask?) It was an overtime game and Meshulam, our playmaker, had come up with this terrific variation of the "pass and go" type of ball we usually play. He brought the ball down the court as I positioned myself under the basket. He faked right to Rosen and then left to Prushner. Both were playing pretty far back and that meant the other team was moving up their defense. That was the plan. Everyone moves away from the net, I get a fast pass and "dunk" right into the basket.

That was the plan.

But you know the story about the best laid plans of mice and men…. Or better yet, the saying, "Man plans and God does His thing." Well, there should be another saying, "Kids make plays and Moms destroy them."

Number 8 from the other team must have seen me heading for the basket from the corner of his

eye. So, he falls back trying to not-so-gently shove me out-of-bounds. He pushes backwards, I push forwards. That's how the game goes sometimes. Of course, Meshulam was having a hard time seeing me behind number 8. And time was running out. So, I try to run around number 8 and get in front of him. Only, number 8 blocks me with his elbow and I feel a shooting pain in my ribs as his elbow gets lodged in my rib cage.

Now, normally, since I had one step ahead of him, I'd forget about number 8's elbow and finish my maneuver. And that's what I tried to do. I ran around number 8, Meshulam fired the ball at me, I caught it, jumped up, turning around in mid-air as I held the ball above my head, ready to shoot it into the basket. Piece of cake.

"FOUL! FOUL ON NUMBER 8!" screeches a voice through a bull horn. "GET OUT OF THE GAME, NUMBER 8! NOW!!"

All the action stopped. Tell you the truth, I thought God was speaking. It was so loud a couple of the guys actually hit the ground, thinking it was some sort of warning. These days you can never be sure that some crazed terrorist won't blow himself up at a game or major event, especially when two Jewish schools are playing against each other. And the way that crazy person said "Number 8" sounded a lot like "Allah Achbar!" the cry of the terrorists before they blow themselves up.

Anyway, it wasn't a crazy person—there are

42
·CHAMPION·

those who would disagree. It was just my Mom. With six of my siblings.

Number 8 must have thought God was speaking to him too, because he ran to his team's bench. I had thrown the ball just as the terrible sound emerged, but I was so scared it flew over the basket, over the backboard, and ended up lodged in one of the rafters in the ceiling.

The refs—there were two of them—didn't really know what to do. There was no law against cheering. But that didn't stop them from shouting up to my mother (she was high up in the stands), "Lady, that's illegal and if you do it once more, we'll throw you out."

Did they really think they could scare a mother with eleven children? Mom just looked them both in the eye and shouted back, "Show me where it says I can't shout through a bullhorn? If you can't do your job, someone has to do it for you. Didn't you see that number 8 jab my son, who was about to win the game for us?"

The refs called time out, and went into a huddle.

Each team went back to their bench and huddled with their coach.

Mom huddled with the kids.

"Silverstein," my coach whispered between

clenched teeth, as we all huddled together. "You better speak to your Mom. If we lose another game, especially this game, because of her, I don't care how well you play, I'll Crazy Glue you to the bench. Permanently. Now get up there."

"Hey, coach," I protested, "those technicals during the last game weren't all my mother's fault. The refs were against us from the start."

"You're darn right they were against us," the coach answered, speaking louder now. "They were against us because your mother led a choir of your brothers and sisters singing "Boo Ref Boo!" to six sets of bongos. It almost gave us a technical!"

I was going to continue to protest, but I wanted to play. So I went up to see Mom.

"Hi Mom," I said, smiling.

"Chutzpah!" she declared. "What a *zets* he gave you with his elbow. The ref must have been blind not to see it. Lift up your shirt, Daniel, let him see your bruise. Go ahead, lift up your shirt." She tried to raise my shirt, but I moved back.

"Come on, Mom. This is basketball. Everyone gets elbowed."

"Does that make it right?" she retorted.

"No, but it's up to the ref to call it. You can't shout like that, using a bullhorn yet. The refs will get angry at our team and we'll lose points. Do you want that?"

"Of course not," Mom answered, softening a bit. "But what are we supposed to teach our children,"

she said, looking at my siblings who played their parts and looked back at her like angels waiting for an assignment. "What's right is right."

"Okay, Mom," I agreed. "You were right. But please, no more bullhorns or groggers or bongos or anything that makes noise. One more time and the coach is going to bench me, permanently."

"We'll see about that," she told me. "Okay, we'll all be quiet. But tell those refs to look at the game. Not at each other. And not at me," she added, for good measure.

The game went on pretty uneventfully after that. Of course Mom shouted, and led her Oreos Choir, as she called them, in the traditional "Defense! Defense! Defense!" when the M&Ms had the ball, and led the atonal "aaAAAAAAAAAAA!" when the M&Ms were about to shoot. Mind you, she did this while diapering Shira, our youngest choir member who sometimes squealed or cried even when our team had the ball. And her thermoses of hot water, hot tea, and hot chocolate were constantly being circulated among the kids, as were the potato chips, candies, and Soup In A Cup. Mom was nothing if not an organizer and she made sure everyone ate and enjoyed themselves, whether they wanted to or not.

Did I mention that we had two technicals called

against us? One was Mom's fault, of course. The other was against me, not because I did anything, but because the refs now knew who Mom's son was. I sort of expected that. I also knew that unless someone took a real big swing at me on the court, the refs were never going to call a foul against me. Unfortunately, eventually the other team understood that as well and it was open season on yours truly.

I saw Mom get up once or twice when I was fouled, but I gave her my "Please! Please! Don't get me into any more trouble!" look and she sat down. She understood that the refs were baiting her. But I hope you don't think Mom let the refs have the last word. Not Mom. Whenever she felt there was a bad call against our team, Mom lined up the kids and had them stick out their tongues at the ref. Mom called this *Mama Loshen* which means "Mama's Tongue." I could see the frustration in the refs' faces. So could everyone else. And the laughter that ensued was infectious.

You know how sometimes everything is going against you and you still come out on top? My Mom says that's God's way of showing us that we don't really know what the future will bring. Unfortunately, that wasn't God's plan.

In the last two minutes of the last quarter, we were down two points. Two of our starting five had fouled out. By some miracle, I was still in the game. But I had four fouls against me and lots of bruises.

Meshulam (also with four fouls) was bringing

the ball down when he shouted
"Sinai!" which means he was
going down the middle for
a lay-up. I thought he was
crazy. The center was
clogged and the best he
could hope for was a foul. More
likely, someone would steal the ball
from him. But Sinai is Sinai. I moved
way off to the left of the basket, and the other guys
spread out as well, trying to clear the center. It still
didn't look like a good idea to me. But Meshulam is
fast. He faked left, right, and left again. Number 3
guarding him lost his balance. Lucky break (Not what
my mother would say.) Meshulam ran straight down
the middle, made the lay-up, *and* got fouled.

Two shots. One minute, ten seconds left to play.
Meshulam swishes the first one in, we're ahead one
point. He misses the second one and the M&Ms take
the ball down. Only 45 seconds left to play.

What's Mom doing? Well, the tension is high
and I can see her straining at the bit, so to speak.
She would love to bullhorn the other team to king-
dom come. But she somehow keeps control of herself. Instead, she takes out two children's blocks and
begins banging them together. Pretty innocuous for
Mom. Just CLOP! CLOP! CLOP! Steady and strong.
As we shift toward the M&Ms court, I'm thinking
what a really great Mom my Mom is. She under-
stands what's at stake here, and she's willing to play

47
·CHAMPION·

the game, our way.

Then the CLOP! CLOP! CLOP! turns into CLOP! CLOP! CLOP! and then CLOP! CLOP! CLOP! as about fifty sets of blocks begin banging together. It sounds like the Surround Sound you get at the movie theaters. The noise is deafening. I keep looking behind me, expecting a stampede of horses to run me down.

It turns out Mom gave the kids bags of these blocks to give out to everyone in the stands. At the signal, they followed Mom's example.

"Hold on to your shorts!" someone on my team screams. "Mrs. S. is at it again!"

My Mom always says that life is filled with short term goals and long term goals. Sometimes the short term goals seem like long term goals because you work so hard on them. But don't stop. You should never lose sight of your long term goals. Keep going.

I think that means that confusing the team with noise seems like a goal worth working for, but the real goal—the long term goal—is making "yours truly" totally insane.

And Mom never gives up.

Most of us on the court are seeing stars and can't even think of guarding the other team. But that was okay because the M&Ms are too busy holding their ears closed to think of shooting the ball.

At some pre-arranged signal the CLOMPING! stopped. Those of us still able to stand made our

CHAMPION

way to the benches. The rest just lay on the floor, where they dropped.

The buzzer sounds. The game, thank God, is over.

My mother gets up and cheers. Solo.

The refs run up to her and gently, but determinedly march her out of the gym. The kids follow, shouting at the refs. Mom takes it in stride and waves to me. Then shouts to her captors: "Negiah!"

I don't know all the laws of when a man can touch a woman, but I don't think the laws of negiah apply to this situation. It's something I'll have to ask the rabbi.

Anyway, the refs come back, give us two retroactive technicals (Is that legal?) and declare the M&Ms the winners.

We head for the showers. The coach tries to give us a pep talk, but everyone is too tired to listen, and he seems too tired to put much pep into his talk. Someone is elected to walk Moshe, the youngest member of our team, home. He's a bit shell-shocked, and keeps crying and mumbling something about the smell of horses.

As I'm about to sneak out, the coach calls me. I debate if I'm close enough to the door to walk out and say I never heard him, but something about his questioning voice convinces me that this may not be the best way to go.

"Do you ever want to play basketball again—and I'm talking about, the rest of your life—then you'd better come here." I considered that a rhetorical question and turned around.

"Yes, coach," I smiled, watching everyone quickly file out.

"Traitor," I whispered to Meshulam as he passed, eyes straight ahead of him.

"What exactly happened, Cooper?" he asked, using my full first name. On better days he calls me Chuck. "Or maybe you don't think using shock therapy against your own team is unusual?"

Not much I could say to that, except shake my head and look at my toes.

"Look, Cooper, I like you," the coach continues. I think I see tears in his eyes. "I've never done anything to hurt you or your family, have I?"

"No sir," I answer, still looking at my toes. "You've been—"

"So why does your family hate me? Why, Cooper? I mean if your mother wants me to play you more, all she has to do is ask. And if you don't like the name Oreos, well let your mother tell me what name she likes. I'm sure we can work things out. Don't you think so, Cooper?"

I look up. Yep, there are tears in his eyes, all right. A couple are even lining up to dribble down his cheek.

"She really means well, Coach. It's just she—"

"You play ball like you mean it, Cooper. I appreciate that. So does the team. We all play hard, don't we Cooper?"

"Yes Coach. We—"

"So why is your mother after us?"

"She's not, Coach," I quietly insist.

"Why does she try to destroy us?"

"She really doesn't think of it like—"

"Will she leave the team alone if I quit?" asks the Coach. At first I think this is just his way of being sarcastic, but then I see he's really asking me. The Coach is ready to quit if I say so. A great feeling of power rolls over me. I suddenly understand why the rabbis warn, *Stay away from the seat of power.* I take a deep breath.

"I promise Coach. I promise she'll never do anything like this again. I-I don't know what got into her. She's never been this crazy before. Honest."

The Coach just looks at me until I can't stand his stare any longer.

"I think I'll have a talk with her now, Coach. Don't worry, everything will be all right."

But the Coach is just staring at me. I turn around, expecting him to say something, something nasty. But instead, I feel his stare on the back of my neck. It's scary. As I leave the gym, I hear the lights

51
·CHAMPION·

shut down. It's totally dark in the gym but the Coach is still standing there, watching me. I know it. I feel it.

Weird.

Did I mention that my Mom is very handy around the house?

One Sunday she decided to "putter around the house," as she calls it, and ended up building me some basketball shelves to store my growing collection of basketballs. Each shelf has three basketball rims and nets screwed into it. But while the rims are real, the nets are made of some sort of strong metal wiring that gives it a 3-D effect. One shelf is horizontal and one vertical. I can throw a ball from anywhere in the room and, if I'm on, swish it into a basket. The horizontal ones are pretty easy, but the vertical baskets are real hard. You have to have just the right touch so they don't bounce out of the basket, since the shelf acts like a backboard. Now is that cool or what?

Mom seems to have a handle on electrical wiring, plastering, and even woodworking. She says that's because when you grow up in a family of nine and have your own family of eleven you soon realize that if you don't fix things yourself they don't get fixed.

If you were a parent reading this story you'd be thinking, "Where do they get the money to send their kids to yeshiva?"

That would be a good question. You need about a gazillion dollars to send eleven kids to yeshiva. You need about half that to provide those same eleven kids with the after school lessons and tutors. Most families would be broke by now, especially since Mom doesn't work. She says, "I never took typing so I can't use a computer. I have no time to be a doctor or lawyer. So what's left?"

I suppose if you can't type, it would make working with computers a little difficult. But whenever anyone has trouble with the hardware in a computer, Mom somehow figures out how to fix it. It's like those old Star Trek movies on television. Scotty, the engineer is always fixing the Enterprise, even though it doesn't look like he knows what's going on in the ship or how to work the engines. That's my Mom. She may not know how to start a computer but she sure can fix 'em. She's our "Scotty" and whenever anything breaks, falls apart, or doesn't work, she always manages to "start the engines."

Which brings me back to the original question: How my family can afford to send us to yeshiva? Simple. Mom fixes everything in the yeshiva, and what doesn't need fixing she changes, and what doesn't need changing—isn't worth keeping. Which means Mom is indispensable.

I remember, when Mom was pregnant with Shira, our eleventh, and had to be in bed two weeks before she gave birth. They almost cancelled school. The bell that signaled when class began and ended kept ringing every five minutes and no one could fix it. One of the vending machines starting giving Coke and Diet Sprite for free whenever anyone hit the left side of the machine, and no one could fix it. Class elections were being held in the auditorium and the sound system blew, as did the lights, and no one could fix them either. And for me, the worst was when our team was due to play an away game and we had no team outfits because my mother was in charge of cleaning the team's clothes. The list went on.

In short, my mother was in charge of almost everything in the school, except the teaching, and even then, when the school was in a pinch for a substitute "who ya gonna call?" Mom.

I heard there was a big debate between the Principal and the Coach regarding Mom and the Basketball Finals. The Coach, in an impassioned plea begged the Principal to declare my mother "persona non grata." I don't know what that means, but I can guess it means something like "The only way she gets into the gym during the Finals is over my dead body!" He wanted a "Silverstein Rule" created which would prohibit anyone named Silverstein from com-

ing to a final, unless he was playing in the game. The Principal tried to point out that such a rule was illegal and the school could be sued. Plus, there was the fact that there were two other Silversteins in the school, not related to me.

The Coach finally threatened to quit if the Principal allowed my mother to come to the Final game (Did I mention we made it to the Finals, losing only that one game against the M&Ms?). The Principal called the Coach's bluff, and the Coach backed down. Some people say that the Principal stood his ground "on principle." Personally, I think he was afraid the school would fall down around his head if my mother wasn't there to help out. In any event, the Coach didn't quit and my mother was allowed to attend the game.

But there was a catch…or two.

The Finals. We were very excited of course. Mom had been talking about nothing else except the game for the last week. She had even waited on line to buy 11 reserved seats. I suppose, thinking back now, I should have thought there was something funny when she came home and announced:

"Your Coach actually had the school put away

11 reserved seats for us. And at half price yet! Wasn't that nice. I think I may have misjudged him."

Mom wasted no time doing her own coaching. She specialized in teaching the kids Cheerleading Techniques, High Pitched Noise Making, Face Scrunching, Name Calling, and gave a Top Secret class which I was not allowed to take part in or even see, called Planned Hysteria.

"Mom," I warned, "the Coach may not be able to keep you from the game, but the refs won't think twice about throwing you out. And remember, we're playing the M&Ms for the Championship this time and the same refs will be on the court. They'll be gunning for you, Mom. Don't make it easy for them."

"Don't worry sweetheart," she assured me. "I'm prepared for every eventuality. We'll obey the rules. I guarantee it."

I wish I could say I believed her. I know you're supposed to believe your Mom, but....

I remember seeing a TV movie about a group of earthlings who land on what they believe to be an uninhabited planet. They set down their spaceship in a valley and start walking up a mountain. When they get to the top of the mountain they stand there, amazed—no, stunned! In front of them is a perfect small American town complete with a grocery store, a drug store, a barber shop, a post office, and everything else you could imagine in Small Town, USA.

They rush down the mountain, eager to meet the people who inhabit this town. But when they get to the town, it's empty. A ghost town.

Suddenly, a metal cage falls over the town, almost blocking out the sun. The spacemen look up, squinting, and see giant faces looking at them. Giant kids appear. There's lots of talking in a strange language. The camera fades and you see that the town in the cage is actually on a high pedestal. In front of the cage is a sign which reads: HUMANS IN THEIR NATURAL HABITAT.

Well, that's about what happened to Mom, and my siblings, when they entered the gym. The ushers (actually security people) gathered my family up and led them to some great front row seats in the middle of the gym. Everyone got comfortable. And then the "ushers" quickly placed a metal cage all around my family.

"Foul!" Mom shouted.

"Kidnapping!" Mom yelled.

"Call the police!" Mom demanded.

The Coach went into "The Pen" as he affectionately called it, and had a few words with my Mom. Instead of chewing him out, she actually looked cowed, shaking her head from side to side and sometimes up and down, not saying a word. Finally, the

Coach smiled and stuck out his hand as though say-ing "Is it a deal?" That's the only time my mother looked him in the eye, staring until the smile on his face disappeared. He put his hand inside his pocket. The Coach realized that he should have known that my mother, a religious woman, would not shake his hand, and I think he felt a little embarrassed. But my mother didn't shout anymore and she seemed to accept her situation.

I was dying to ask the Coach what he said, but we were getting ready for the big pep talk, and filed into the locker room.

"Gentlemen," the Coach began, "I don't have to tell you how important this game is to me—to all of us. We've worked hard, and," here the Coach looked directly at me, "we've had some major disap-pointments. But we've learned one thing: If we work together we're unbeatable!" Now, everyone looked at me, and I was sure they were thinking of Mom.

"So, what do we have to do now?"

"Win!" shouted the team.

"What?" repeated the Coach.

"Win!" we all shouted, louder. I could feel the adrenaline pumping.

"And who are we going to beat?" yelled the Coach.

"M&M!"

"Who's going to melt in our hands?" continued the Coach.

"M&M!" went the hysterical response.

"And who's going to flat-
ten the M&Ms?"

"The Oreos!"

"Who?" the Coach
asked, as though hard of
hearing.

"The Oreos!" we screamed.

"Go get 'em!" the Coach commanded.

And away we flew onto the court.

I'm not going to bore you with the first half of
the game. The only really outstanding moments were
when Sammy slipped—we thought he was fouled—
and had to be taken off the court. He was in the
starting five and he was the rebound king of the
league. You could hear us gulp in unison as we saw
him being carried out. Someone said his leg was
broken. We lost ten points in succession after that
but by the end of the second quarter Sammy was
back. It had only been a sprain after all and he felt
fine. In no time, we made up the points.

The other memorable moment was when I lost
my kippah on the court. I know you don't see players
wearing a kippah or any headgear on television (it's
probably illegal), but in our league lots of kids wear
kippot. Actually, we do this thing after a time-out
where the guy with the biggest kippah (that's usually
Stevie) gets into the middle of our circle and we all

put our hands on his kippah. One guy (usually me) shouts "What are you gonna hit 'em with?" and everyone answers "Oreos!"

Now, all of us with kippot make sure to wear these little clips that keep a kippah attached to your hair. And the refs (even those not Jewish) know that if a kippah falls off a kid's head they should just pick it up and wait until after the play is finished. Then they give the kid his kippah back. But sometimes, the plays come together so fast everyone forgets about the kippah.

Not my mother.

I was running down court with the ball and an M&M jumped in front of me, daring me to charge him. I stopped short but my kippah kept going—right into the guy's face. He took it and threw it aside. Not a very religious or respectful thing to do, I admit, but in the middle of the game no one is thinking religion or respect. They're thinking blood. So, he throws my kippah out of the court near a player from his team. Not on purpose, mind you. The other player picks it up and flings it way up into the stands. On purpose.

Me and the guy guarding me have no idea what is going on. I'm looking to pass to someone and he's looking to block me or take away the ball.

Suddenly, I hear a scream.

"*Apikores!*" Mom shouts.

"Heretic!" Mom yells.

"Throw him out!" Mom demands.

60

CHAMPION

Both coaches call time out and both refs blow their whistles. I begin to think about joining the school ping pong team or playing solitaire for the rest of my adolescent life—anything that will keep *Mom the Killer Fan* out of my life.

The coach marches into The Pen and confronts Mom. My team is sitting on the bench and I'm trying to keep a low profile.

"Your Mom again, huh Silverstein," one of the guys mumble.

"If we lose this game because of your Mom, Cooper," my friend Meshulam whispers, "I *will* kill you. And you know the best part of it, I won't have to plead insanity. They'll consider it a mercy killing. I'll be doing you and the team a major favor."

"How did you get into that family, Cooper?" Morris asks.

"Adoption," I suggest.

"Go back to the kennel," someone quips.

The coach comes back, trying not to look at me.

"Okay, here's the plan," he says. But everyone is looking at Mom in The Pen. She's handing out popcorn to the kids in there with her. She seems happy, and the kids are all smiling. "Pay attention, everyone," he orders. "We only have three minutes

until half-time and we're two points down. Here's the way we work it...."

While everyone's studying the play, I sneak a glance at Mom. She sees me and waves. I can't understand why she's so happy.

"Krevitz, you take Silverstein's spot. Remember to break when Meshulam gives you the sign. Now everyone, let's do it!"

I'm hoping the Coach took me out to give me some rest, but I know in my heart of hearts he's just punishing me because of Mom.

"Okay, Cooper, here's the deal," the Coach tells me. "Your mother and me have an agreement," he smiles, pointing to my Mom.

"My Mom made an agreement with you?" I sort of echo.

"You see, Silverstein, I told her that if she does anything—and I mean anything—wrong from now until the end of the game, I will have you sit out the game. I don't care if we lose. And if everyone—I mean, everyone—fouls out in this game, I will rather forfeit the game than put you in."

"What did she say?" I wondered out loud.

"Okay."

"Okay?" I asked. "Just—okay?"

"Yeah. So, now I'm putting you into the game. But if your Mom does one more lamebrained stunt or forces the refs to blow their whistle one more time, you'll be sitting out the rest of the game, and probably, the rest of your life. Is that clear?"

I nod.

"Okay, now just to make sure it's okay, I want you to walk over to your Mom and tell her what I just told you."

I looked at the Coach, hardly believing my ears. No one ever walked over to their mother during a game. It just wasn't done. And I certainly didn't want to break a tradition like that.

"I trust you, Coach," I told him.

"But I don't trust her. Do it," he insisted.

So, I walk to my Mom, feeling like all eyes are on me. I sneak into The Pen. My mother and the kids look like they've been expecting me.

"Mom, you've got to help me out, here," I say, almost crying.

"Don't worry, dear, I've taken care of everything. Trust me, it will all work out."

Those two terrible words made me flinch. "Trust me," was a sure recipe for disaster.

"Mom, he's going to bench me, permanently if you do anything wrong," I warn her.

"I know. And that's why you have to trust me," she says again, smiling.

All the kids were smiling too. What do they know that I don't know?

"Go now, sweetheart," Mom orders, first pushing me towards her and planting a big kiss on my cheek. "You be your usual great self. We have everything under control," she assures me.

If I wasn't nervous before, I am nervous and terrified now. Everyone is smiling, just like the time I came down for breakfast, late as usual. Everyone had been waiting for the last kid to come down to breakfast (who likes to be first in the morning?) and have a traditional bowl of cornflakes. I thought it was funny that I didn't have to fight anyone for the cereal. They were all eating different things for a change. How was I to know that there was a big S for *Sucker* written on my forehead. I took a bowl, poured the cornflakes, added milk, took a big spoonful and— Sneezed! I sneezed my head off. I accidentally (actually, it was an involuntary hand swing brought about by the sneezing) turned over the milk carton and flipped the bowl onto the floor.

"I suppose that proves your theory," Mom told Izzy, between laughs. "Now you can tell your teacher you were right."

I didn't stay around long enough to find out what the "theory" was all about. I sneezed myself into the bathroom and from there out the door and then onto the bus. I was still sneezing when the third period bell rang.

So, I was not happy to see all these smiling faces.

"Trust me!" kept echoing in my head. I wondered if that was the last thing the spider said to the fly, as she spun her web around him.

"Time out!" the Coach calls with just 30 seconds to play. I substitute Prushner.

I take out the ball and pass to my left. 20 seconds left to play and I've got the ball again. No one is free. The M&Ms are guarding us tight. So, I fake to my left and plow down the middle for a lay-up. Pow! Whack! I'm fouled by about a dozen hands but somehow manage to get the shot in, and the two foul shots that follow. When the half-time buzzer rings, we're 2 points up.

What can I tell you. I was wrong. We were all wrong. Mom and the kids clapped and whistled, but no more than the other fans. Mom and the kids booed and hissed the other team, but no more than the other fans. Mom and the kids stomped their feet and banged on their seats, but no more than the other fans.

And for 28 minutes and 22 seconds of the second half, they were the perfect fans. I only wish we would have been the perfect team.

During the third quarter Sammy, our star rebounder starts limping. His earlier sprain is obviously more serious than anyone thought and he hobbles off the court for good. Krevitz fouls out by the end of the third quarter and so one of our best

shooters is gone. Midway through the fourth quarter our fast-breaking forward, Yahnkee, steals the ball, races down court and, as he's making the lay-up, trips over his own shoelaces and crashes onto the floor, knocking himself out.

When was the last time you saw that?

I'd love to say that I, Chuck-Cooper Silverstein single-handedly saved the day, but it just ain't so. I played okay, even great at times, but as a team, the Oreos had lost their filling. We were being squashed by the M&Ms.

One minute and forty-eight seconds left to play in the game and we're about twenty-two points down. It could have been more. I stopped looking at the points display soon after Yahnkee KO'd himself. I just glanced at the clock on the wall every ten seconds, praying for the end of the game.

And my prayers were heard.

With exactly one minute and forty-eight seconds left to play, the lights on the court went out. Twenty seconds later the emergency sprinkler system activated and it started raining—indoors. Somehow the loudspeakers were still working and our team song, "One Tough Cookie" was blaring. No one really panicked. Then, miraculously, the lights went back on and the emergency sprinklers shut off. But by then the floor had two inches of water covering it and almost everyone had scrambled out of the gym.

The game, of course, had to be cancelled due to (indoor) rain. Which was fine by us. The rule in

our league is that championship games have to be played
through. That means, if
the game is called off for
whatever reason, you
have to start again. Which
meant we got another chance at
the M&Ms.

The game is scheduled for next
Sunday.

I know what you're thinking. Mom did it. But
I've got to tell you, there is no proof whatsoever, and
don't think there weren't plenty of people who wanted
to pin it on her. We had the city inspectors come
and check the wiring of the gym. They couldn't find
a thing. It was, in their own words, "a one-time
fluke."

The only thing that sort of bothers me is that
the Coach and Mom are suddenly such good friends.
The Coach even lets Mom sit in on practices, something he would never do before. When I asked the
Coach how come he's getting along so well with Mom,
he just smiled and said, "We have an agreement,
your mother and I."

And when I asked my mother the same thing,
she just said, "That Coach of yours is a very good
person. You should learn from him."

Go figure.

Oh yes, there is one other thing that bothers
me a bit. When the lights went on and the sprin-

CHAMPION

klers went off, I could have sworn I saw my mother and the kids quickly put away umbrellas.

But it was crazy right then and it was hard to see into The Pen, what with everyone running around.

And anyway, why would they bring umbrellas to an indoor basketball game?

THE SEVENTH INNING BOMB

BY AVRAHAM BERGER

Avraham Berger

(8) As a boy growing up in Ohio, my favorite sport was baseball. At every opportunity, from April through September, I would either be playing baseball, talking about it, or following the progress of my home team, the Cleveland Indians. The great American pastime was indeed my favorite pastime.

As an adult, I made Jerusalem my home. Life is very good here, but for the past few years we have had a terrible problem with terrorism. Suicide bombers have brought death and sadness to our city. Many good people have been killed by these monsters.

In this story I focus on these two periods of my life that are separated by many years and many miles. The game of my youth meets the current problem facing me.

THE SEVENTH INNING BOMB

It was a Saturday night in Jerusalem. Yigal, Kobi, and Ron were walking down Ben Yehuda Street, going to a birthday party. Their classmate, Yossi Marcus, had just turned twelve, and his parents had invited them, his three best friends, to join the family at a local restaurant to celebrate.

"I love parties", said Yigal. "It's always fun to get out of the house and meet with friends, especially on a happy occasion."

"But it's so cold tonight", complained Kobi. "Wouldn't you rather be at home, wrapped in a warm blanket? There's a great movie on TV tonight. And our refrigerator is full of leftovers from the Shabbat meals. Why did Yossi have to have a birthday party tonight?"

"And what about Palestinian terrorists?" asked Ron. "There have been so many attacks lately. Just thinking about them makes me nervous."

Yigal, the eternal optimist, spoke up. "Come on, guys. So what if it's a little cold? We're tough. Yossi's parents invited us to a party. We can't disappoint them. Getting together with friends is a lot more fun than sitting in front of a stupid TV. And that is especially true if the party is in a good restaurant. I can already taste that fat, juicy hamburger that I'm going to order. And no terrorist is going to scare me.

71
·CHAMPION·

This is my country, and I'll go where I want. We're not babies who can be pushed around. Now let's go have a good time."

As usual, Yigal's enthusiasm proved to be contagious. Ron and Kobi put their negativity aside, and began getting into a party mood.

Not many people were in town on this cold winter night. As they turned off Ben Yehuda to the side street where the restaurant was, Yigal noticed three men standing in the shadows. Suddenly, a street light that had been dark lit up, giving Yigal a clear look at their faces. They were all Palestinians, about twenty years of age. But just as this information was registering in his mind, the boys arrived at the restaurant. As they entered, they saw Yossi, and began to yell: "Happy Birthday!" Everyone in the restaurant turned towards the birthday boy, and added their own greetings.

When the boys were seated, everyone at the table ordered the specialty of the house, hamburgers with french fries. With that taken care of, the entertainment part of the birthday festivities began. Sara, Yossi's eight-year-old sister read a poem that she had composed. The poem described how creepy Yossi was, but that she loved him anyway.

Next on the agenda were the three friends. As they stood up and faced their audience, they looked almost like triplets. Each of them was about five foot five and slim, with short brown hair. The only one who looked somewhat different was Yigal, with his

piercing eyes, and radiant smile. Yigal, Kobi, and Ron proceeded to sing a song that they had written for the occasion. In ten long verses, they praised Yossi's many virtues and talents, in three part harmony. As the song came to an end, everyone cheered and clapped loudly. And then they clapped even louder as the food arrived.

Yigal was just about to bite into his hamburger, when....

KABOOOOOOOM!!!!!!!!!!

What happened? Let me think. It's so hard to concentrate. Wait! There was a terribly loud noise. Broken glass is everywhere. People are screaming. There are sirens and flashing lights. I can't move my right arm. I'm bleeding. What is going on????

Yigal opened his eyes. Where was he? Why was he here? The last thing he remembered was sitting in a restaurant with his buddies. Now he was in bed, in a strange room, with machines all around him. When he tried to sit up, he felt a sharp pain in his right shoulder. Turning his head to that side, he saw that the shoulder was covered with bandages. Everything he saw confused him, until he noticed his mother sitting in a chair next to his bed, asleep.

"Mom," he whispered.

Karen Goldstein opened her eyes and turned to the bed. For the first time in three days, her twelve-year-old son was awake. He was looking at her.

"Yigal!" she screamed, and hugged the boy. She began sobbing hysterically as she held him, and kept repeating the words: "Thank God" over and over.

After several minutes, Yigal's mother regained her composure. She explained to her son where he was, and what had happened.

"We are in the orthopedic department of Hadassah Hospital", began Karen. "You were in a terrorist attack. A suicide bomber exploded a bomb outside the restaurant where you and your friends were having the party. Many people were injured. The blast knocked you out, and injured your right shoulder."

"What happened to my friends?" asked Yigal. "Are they okay? And what about Yossi's family?"

Karen took Yigal's hand, and held it firmly. "I'm sorry Yigal. Yossi and Kobi are dead. Ron is alive, but his legs were severely hurt. We don't know if he'll ever walk again. Yossi's parents and sisters were lucky. They only had minor injuries."

Yigal stared at the ceiling, trying to absorb what his mother had just told him. "Yossi and Kobi are dead? Ron can't walk? Ron was the fastest runner in our whole school. Oh God. Oh God! How could this have happened? Why did this happen? Wait! I saw them. I saw three Palestinians standing near the restaurant. Those must be the ones who carried

out the attack. When I saw them, I knew that something was wrong. I knew that they shouldn't be there. But I didn't do anything about it. I should have told a policeman, but instead I just ignored them. I didn't pay attention, and went into the restaurant. If I would have acted and gotten a policeman, my friends would be alive today. Oh God. I deserve to be lying here injured. I killed them. I could have saved them, but didn't. It's my fault. I LET MY FRIENDS DIE. I LET MY FRIENDS DIE!"

Overwhelmed by pain, loss, and guilt, Yigal began screaming and crying. His mother held him tightly. "Yigal, you can't be sure that those Palestinians were the ones who set off the bomb," she yelled into his ear. But Yigal would not listen, and would not be comforted. If anything, his crying intensified. "I let them die! My friends are dead! I did it! I did it!" The only thing that calmed him down was an injection of a sedative, which the nurse, rushing in, administered.

Over the next several days, Yigal had two operations on his right shoulder. Two weeks after the attack, he left the hospital and went home. After four months of physical therapy, he could use his right arm almost as well as before the attack. As the school year came to an end, Yigal had regained his health. But this twelve-year-old boy who had always

·CHAMPION·

been noisy, fun loving, and interested in everything, had stopped talking, and didn't have energy for anything other than staring at the TV.

"Abba, Ima, I would like to talk to you."

Benny and Karen Goldstein, Yigal's parents, looked up in surprise. Since the terrorist attack Yigal had not initiated a single conversation. In fact, in all these months, he had barely said a word to anyone.

"I know that since the attack, I've acted like a zombie. It used to be that you couldn't stop me from blabbering. Now, I have nothing to say to anyone. The reason is that I'm ashamed. I'm so ashamed that I can't look anyone in the face. I can't even look at myself in the mirror. If I had called for a policeman on that terrible night, the attack might have been prevented, and my friends would still be alive."

"We've been over this many times," his father interrupted. "You don't even know that those three Palestinians were involved. You can't even be sure they were Palestinians."

Yigal continued. "Maybe. But deep in my heart, I still blame myself. And you would too.

"So, I've made a decision. I want to go away for a while. I want to be in a place where no one knows me, and no one knows how I have failed. India or Brazil would be perfect. But I know that you wouldn't agree to a trip like that. So, as a compromise, I'm asking that you let me spend the summer with Uncle Jimmy and his family in America. School ended today, so I have vacation for all of July and August.

76

CHAMPION

Can I go?"

As his parents silently considered his request, the same thoughts occurred to both of them. A person shouldn't run away from a problem. But on the other hand, life in Israel was just aggravating his trauma, and with nothing to think about all summer, he would just mope and become more depressed in Israel.

"It's fine with me," his mother said. "What do you think, dear?"

"It's fine with me," his father echoed. "But there is one condition. I don't want you sitting in America vegetating. While you're there, you have to take part in all the activities that your cousins take part in."

"Agreed," Yigal intoned, with little enthusiasm.

A week later, Yigal made the long journey from Israel to New York, to northeastern Ohio. As he got off the plane at Cleveland Hopkins Airport, he let out a sigh of relief. "Maybe here I'll be able to forget," he thought.

As Yigal waited at the luggage carousel to get his suitcase, he saw his Uncle Jimmy approaching. Jimmy, his father's older brother, had always been his favorite uncle. Whenever he came to visit them in Jerusalem, he would bring wonderful gifts, and tell fantastic stories. Everyone loved Uncle Jimmy.

77

CHAMPION

But now, as the uncle with the ever-smiling face came near, an inner voice whispered, *he knows that because of you, your friends are dead.*

A wave of embarrassment broke over Yigal, as it had so many times in Israel. "Why did I come here?" he asked himself. In those few seconds his mood turned sour.

Seeing the gloomy look on Yigal's face, Jimmy realized that the boy was depressed, so he just patted him on the back, said hello, and helped him bring his luggage into the car. He didn't bother Yigal with small talk.

They drove to the Cleveland suburb of Mayfield Heights in silence. As they pulled into the driveway, they were greeted by Aunt Betty, and his twin cousins Joey and Mark. When Yigal got out of the car, Aunt Betty embraced him, and smothered him with kisses. The cousins smiled, slapped him on the back, and began to barrage him with questions.

"How was your trip? Was there good food on the plane? How many movies did they show?"

Yigal just frowned at them, and mumbled under his breath. He looked so unhappy that his aunt and cousins thought that they had done something to offend him. Jimmy understood what the problem was, and suggested that they go inside and have something to eat. But Yigal declined, said that he was tired, and asked if he could go to sleep. They were disappointed, but what could they do? Betty took Yigal to his room.

After Betty got their guest settled in his bedroom, she came downstairs, and found the family sitting in the den, all with sad faces.

"What's wrong with him?" asked Joey. "He was always the liveliest boy I knew."

"Yeah," Mark seconded. "Every time we visited him in Israel, the last thing he wanted to do was go to bed. He dragged us from one fun activity to another. We could hardly keep up with him. He was the life of the party."

"You have to realize," said Jimmy, "that Yigal had a terrible shock. He was just a few feet from a terrorist bomb when it exploded. To wake up in a hospital and find out that two of your best friends were dead, and that another would never walk again is more that anyone should have to deal with.

"Boys, we have a job to do. Yigal is going to be with us for the next two months. We want to send him back to Israel as a happier boy than he is now. Are we all agreed on this point?"

Everyone nodded.

"So here is the plan. Starting tomorrow, you boys are going to introduce him to the great game of baseball. You're going to show him how the game is played. You'll teach him batting and fielding. His father always tells me how good he is in soccer and basketball. If he can play those sports, he can learn baseball. I'm hoping that through baseball, he will regain his self-confidence. Any questions?" Uncle Jimmy waited a moment to make sure the boys understood what was expected of them. "So, do you boys know what you have to do?

"Play ball!" they both shouted in unison.

The next morning, when Yigal came to the breakfast table, he found his two cousins totally involved in the sports page of the local newspaper. They were having a lively discussion about the previous night's baseball game. The mood was festive because the Cleveland Indians had beaten the Boston Red Sox by a score of 4 to 0. As Yigal sat down, Betty put a bowl of cornflakes in front of him. But the boys didn't even notice that he was there. Since Yigal's parents were born in Cleveland, and English was the spoken language in his house, he had no difficulty communicating with his American relatives. But Mark and Joey were now speaking in a language that was completely foreign to him. Runs, hits, fielding, strike outs—what were they talking about? And they were so excited!

"What are the two of you talking about?" asked Yigal. "I don't understand a single word you're saying."

"The Indians just swept a three game series from the Red Sox", said Mark. "Last night's game was a shutout. Bob Wickman pitched a 2 hitter, and Jim Thome won it for us with a grand slammer in

the ninth. It was great!"

"Slow down", pleaded Yigal. "I still don't understand what you're talking about."

"Elementary, dear Yigal", said Joey. "We are talking about the great American past time— baseball. There isn't a single boy in this country who doesn't love this game. From the start of spring, until the rain of autumn, this is what we do. And when we aren't playing it, we watch the professional teams slug it out. Our local team is the Cleveland Indians. They haven't won a World Series since 1948, but we never stop hoping. Oh, you probably don't know what the World Series is. It's the championship series. What do you call it in soccer? World Cup? Mondial? Anyway, that's our hope, to see the Indians in the World Series."

Yigal was trying to absorb all of this when Joey asked him: "You do play baseball, don't you?"

"No. I've never played it. I've never even seen it played. I don't know anything about this game," admitted Yigal.

"Well cousin," said Mark, "you've got a lot of learning ahead of you. This is what we do all summer. Your first lesson starts right after breakfast."

The three boys walked out of the Goldstein family home, armed with bats, gloves, a softball, and a proper amount of cookies and candy. Each of them wore a Cleveland Indians baseball cap, with the visor curled and molded to show they were seasoned ball players. In the heat of the Ohio summer, they walked three blocks to the park that had several baseball diamonds. As they walked, the lecture began:

Nine players to a team, nine innings to a game.

Three strikes and you're out.

Infield, outfield.

Home plate, first base, second base, third base.

Home run, line drive, fly ball, foul ball....

When they got to the park, they sat on the grass near a game in progress, and explained to Yigal what was going on. As the time passed, the Israeli cousin began to catch on. After an hour, the game they were watching was over, their supply of goodies was gone, and it was time to get up and start throwing the ball around.

"OK, Yigal, enough talking. This is a mitt. You catch the ball with it. It goes on your left hand."

"But I'm right handed", protested Yigal. "Shouldn't I wear it on my right hand?"

"Good question", said Mark, "but the answer is no. If you are right handed, that is the hand you want to throw with. You can't throw with a glove on your right hand, so it goes on the left."

The cousins stood about 15 feet from each other, and began to slowly throw the ball around. At first, Yigal had a hard time judging the path of the ball

approaching him, so he either ended up getting hit by the ball, or missing it completely. But slowly, the coordination came, and he began to correctly position the glove and make the catch.

Next came batting. They were playing with a softball, so the pitching was underhand. But it proved to be very difficult for poor Yigal. After he swung and missed for the twentieth time in a row, he threw the bat to the ground, and began to walk away in disgust.

"I can't do this", he yelled. "I just can't."

Yigal's walking turned into a run. He began to cry, and the tears streamed down his face. His cousins ran after him, but couldn't keep up with him.

After a while, he slowed down, and the three of them walked silently to the house. Yigal went straight to bed, and slept the rest of the day and through the night.

———————————————————————

The next morning, when Yigal came into the kitchen, his two cousins came over to him.

"I don't think that what happened over there is your fault", said Joey. "If you could have helped your friends, you would have. That monster of a terrorist is the one who did it. You shouldn't be carrying around guilt for what someone else did. You are a swell guy.

83

We're glad that you're our cousin."

Yigal was stunned for a moment. No one had spoken about the attack until now. He realized that everyone had been walking on egg shells and that he needed to change his attitude, for their sake. He started to smile, and the three cousins warmly embraced each other.

After about a minute, Mark spoke up. "Hey! That's enough of this mushy stuff. Let's eat breakfast and get to batting practice. You still swing the bat like an old lady."

The cousins returned to the park. Yigal held the bat and squared off opposite Joey, the pitcher. In came the pitch, a swing, a miss. Mark, the catcher threw the ball back to his brother, and they tried again. And again. And again. After fifty, unsuccessful swings, Mark began to pitch. But like his brother, Mark recorded strike out after strike out. Finally, they took a break from the batting, and went back to throwing and catching practice, which Yigal was doing with reasonable success.

After lunch, the trio worked on batting again. To everyone's surprise, on the very first pitch, Yigal connected and hit a pop fly to the edge of the infield.

"All right!" yelled Joey and Mark, as they danced around the diamond. But Yigal was so surprised that he forgot what to do after hitting the ball. All he could think of was "Wow! I hit it. I hit it. Wow, I hit the ball!

"Don't just stand there," Mark yelled, "run to first base."

Forgetting to drop the bat, Yigal took off for first. Mark ran to field the ball, and Joey went to cover the base. By the time Mark received the throw, Yigal had a stand-up single. His hitting career had begun.

Over the next week, the cousins worked on all of the baseball skills. Slowly but surely, Yigal improved. With improvement came confidence. And with confidence came enthusiasm. With each new success, the young Israeli boy smiled more and more.

One morning, as the boys were finishing breakfast, Mark turned to Yigal and said: "I think you are ready to play. Today we'll go to a different park, and you'll be in a game."

Yigal wasn't so sure. "Do you really think I'm ready?"

"Don't worry. You'll be fine."

Three hours later, as the boys walked home for lunch, Yigal was shaking his head.

"I struck out. I grounded out. I popped out twice. I committed five errors. I told you that I wasn't ready."

Mark didn't agree with Yigal's assessment. "You also hit a double. Besides those errors, your fielding wasn't bad. And your fast running prevented a hard

hit left field grounder from turning into a home run. I'd say that for your first game, you did OK. Don't worry. Tomorrow will be better."

Mark was right. The next day's game was better. As the weeks past, Yigal became as good as many of the other boys his age. Best of all, slowly, the pain of the terrorist bomb was being pushed further into the background.

Yigal's success on the baseball diamond led to social acceptance. He was becoming one of the gang. Encouraged by the camaraderie, his radiant smile began to return. In between games, he told his teammates about life in Israel, and began to teach them Hebrew. Some of the twelve-year-old boys even asked if he would give them Bar Mitzvah lessons. Yigal became the center of attention.

July had been Yigal's month for learning baseball. By August, his cousins felt that he was ready to see how the professionals played. So, on a humid August evening, the Goldstein family took Yigal to see the Cleveland Indians play the New York Yankees at Jacobs Field.

As they entered the ballpark and headed for their seats, Yigal found himself looking everywhere at once, taking in the experience. The giant stadium, the smell of the peanuts and popcorn, the roar of the crowd, all of these put Yigal into the spirit of big league baseball. When the Indians took the field, he

could see himself in left field, punching his fist into the glove, ready to play. The excitement of the game was energizing. Every time the ball was hit, his muscles tightened, as if he were running to first base. Every ball hit to left field was his play. From the stands of Cleveland Stadium, he lived that game as if he were in it. Inning after inning, he was riveted to the action, unaware of those around him. Only at the seventh inning stretch did he remember where he was, smile at his relatives, and stand up to stretch with the other 20,000 fans.

When the stretch was over, the owner of the Indians walked out to the mound with a microphone, and began to make a speech. Yigal and Mark took the opportunity to run out to the refreshment stand and buy some peanuts.

On the way back to their seats, the two cousins discussed one of the particularly exciting innings. They were so engrossed in their conversation that they didn't pay attention to where they were going. Suddenly, they realized that they were lost. As they retraced their steps, Mark heard someone talking in a foreign language that seemed familiar.

"Yigal, listen. I think I hear someone talking Hebrew. It seems to be coming from that storage room," Mark said, pointing.

Yigal moved toward the storage room, straining

to hear the voices. Indeed, the words they were hearing were similar enough to Hebrew to fool Mark. Yigal, on the other hand, realized that they were listening to a different Semitic language, Arabic. Yigal motioned to his cousin to be quiet.

When they reached the storage area Mark opened the door. It was dark and filled with maintenance tools. From somewhere in the darkness, they could hear three men speaking in Arabic. Yigal tried to focus on their conversation.

"The attendance was just announced," one of the men said. "There are over twenty thousand people at tonight's game. This is the opportunity that we have been waiting for. The score is tied, so it is unlikely that anyone will leave early. When the game ends, all the people will move towards the stairways where our explosives are hidden. At just the right moment, BOOM! Those who aren't killed by the explosions or the falling stairs will be crushed in the resulting panic. Thousands will die in a matter of minutes. Allah is great. As our brother, Bin Laden destroyed the great American dream so will we, Hamas, destroy the great American past time.

"I've placed a charge in the main electricity panel. After the explosion, the stadium will be in total darkness. The darkness will cause more panic and slow down the rescue effort, resulting in more deaths.

"The time has come. We'll wait in the car in the stadium parking lot. There we can listen to the

game on the radio. After it ends, when we see the first people leaving the stadium, I'll detonate the first bomb in the electricity panel. Let's go."

As the boys hid, the three terrorists walked out of the dark storage area into the corridors of the stadium. As soon as they were out of sight, Yigal whispered to his cousin, "We have to follow them." The two boys dashed out of the dark area, and immediately caught sight of the three men walking in the direction of the main exit.

"What's going on?" whispered Mark. "What did they say?"

Yigal got straight to the point. "They are members of the Palestinian terror organization called Hamas. When the game is over, they are going to blow up the stadium by remote control. That little box that the taller of the three is carrying must be the detonation device. We have to get it away from him, and alert the police."

"What if they have guns?" asked Mark. "If we try any funny stuff with them, they might shoot us. Maybe we should just find a cop."

"If they see a cop, they'll detonate the bomb," answered Yigal. "They don't know we're aware of their plan. If we don't act right now, a lot of people, including your parents and brother will die. Here's the plan."

Yigal whispered into Mark's ear as they continued walking.

"You're crazy," Mark cried, stopping in his tracks.

"Don't worry", Yigal assured him, pushing him forward. "My plan will work. Go!"

The three Palestinians were about twenty feet ahead of the cousins, walking next to each other. Mark started sprinting to their left, looking back at Yigal who was waving him on. As Mark was about to pass the terrorists, he turned and plowed into the two on the left. The surprise impact knocked them to the ground, with Mark on top of them. Mark instantly jumped up, began screaming, and ran. At the same time, Yigal ran behind the terrorist and grabbed the detonator. He dashed towards the stands, catching up to Mark who was still screaming.

The terrorists gave chase.

Yigal and Mark were now both shouting "Terrorists! Terrorists!" But the game had begun and everyone was standing up to watch a long hit by Jim Thome into left field. It was so noisy that no one except those close to the boys could hear.

As the boys reached the first row of box seats, they jumped over the low wall, entering the playing field. Continuing their mad dash, they ran to the pitcher's mound. There they crashed into the Yankee's pitcher, who was also watching the hit. The sight of two boys on the field and the tackled pitcher caught everyone's attention, especially the police on duty at the game.

The terrorists had also jumped over the wall. Their leader was making a final effort to reach the detonator. He caught Yigal by the back of his jacket, but fell over the pitcher, taking Yigal down with him.

"Mark!" Yigal shouted, tossing the detonator to his cousin just as he fell down. Mark caught the detonator with both hands, careful not to push or pull anything that might set it off. By this time the other two terrorists had reached the mound and were almost on top of him.

"Help!" Mark shouted, and threw the detonator high into the air, towards the second base man. "It's a bomb! Don't let it drop on the ground!" he screamed as both terrorists tackled him.

The second base man lunged forward and caught the detonator inches from the ground. Then, he took his glove off and, with the detonator still in his glove, put it gently on second base. And ran.

Most of the 20,000 fans had no idea what was happening but applauded the spectacular catch of the second base man.

The police converged on the terrorists and the cousins, putting handcuffs on all of them.

By the time Jimmy got onto the field, the policemen had cleared up the confusion and dragged the terrorists out of the stadium.

Because of the potential danger in leaving the

CHAMPION

stadium, or even remaining in the stands, all of the fans and players gathered in the center of the playing field. While they sat there, dozens of police and FBI bomb specialists arrived and combed the stadium, looking for explosives. Two hours later, the twenty thousand fans were sent home. Jimmy and the three cousins were given an escort home.

The next day, Jimmy received a call from the manager of the stadium.

"Listen," he said, "we have a double-header tonight and we'd really like for you all to be our guests. We've got box seats waiting for you. But first, I'd like you to come to my office before the game."

Who could refuse such an offer.

When they arrived, Jimmy and the boys were escorted into one of the stadium offices. There they sat down with the managers of both teams, two officers from the Cleveland Police Department, and three agents of the FBI. Agent Ted Jones, the most senior member of the FBI in Ohio began to speak.

"Yesterday you people saved thousands of lives. We went over every inch of the stadium, and found an enormous quantity of explosives, ready to be detonated by remote control. Had Yigal and Mark not stopped them, the death toll would have been many times greater than 9/11. We are in the process of investigating how such a plot could have been carried out, right under our noses, without anyone discovering it. But one thing is clear," he added, looking at Yigal and Mark, "you two boys prevented a

terrible tragedy from happening, and we are forever grateful."

"No, you've got it wrong," protested Mark. "I barely did anything. Yigal is the hero. He understood what the Hamas terrorists were saying. He devised the plan. He forced me to help him. I was afraid, but he encouraged me. Yigal should get all of the credit."

"I hear what you're saying, Mark," replied Agent Jones. "Yigal, your bravery and quick thinking saved thousands of lives. Is there anything I can do for you?"

Yigal was silent for a moment, and then smiled.

"I have a favor to ask of you. If my parents find out I was mixed up with terrorists, they'll never let me come to the States again. Can we keep what happened tonight a secret?"

"Sorry, Yigal," replied the FBI agent, with a big smile on his face. "I think it's a bit late for that. At this very moment your mother and father are on the phone with the President of the United States. He called them to personally thank them for what their brave son did."

Yigal blushed.

"Oh, before I forget," the manager of the Cleveland Indians said, taking out a baseball, "This is for you." The ball was covered with the names of all the players.

CHAMPION

"And here's one from us," the Yankees manager said, holding up a ball covered with the names of the players. "And here's one more ball," he added. It had nothing on it.

Yigal held the ball in his hand.

"What do I do with it?" he asked.

"You go out there, tonight," the Indians manager told him. "Throw it, and shout—"

"PLAY BALL!" Everyone in the room shouted.

SH'MA!

BY ELIOT FINTUSHEL

95

CHAMPION

Eliot Fintushel

There was a time when I did almost nothing but play chess. I memorized openings and endings and famous games. I carried a pocket chess set with me everywhere I went. I played in tournaments and owned a chess clock and had a shelf full of books and magazines all about chess chess chess. The only thing I didn't like about chess was the way it made all my friends into enemies: I had to win, win, win....

I don't play chess much anymore, but there's enough of chess love left in me, for example, to make me write this story....

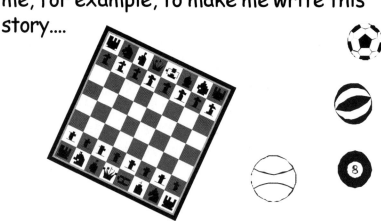

Sh'ma!

My attack gathered strength. One of my rabbis ("bishops," some chess players call them) was trained on G.'s weak corner pawn, while the other pinned the enemy knight against his queen. G. stared at his ruined position. Three more moves, I figured, and the shout of "Sh'ma!" would ring in the air.

When they kill the king, most will crow, "Checkmate," but I liked to say, "Sh'ma!" *Sh'ma* is more electric than "checkmate": it means "Hear!" as in *"Sh'ma Yisroel,"* (Hear, O Israel!). When I played chess, look out! I was the Angel of Death.

G. stared unblinkingly. His sleeve had been resting near the woodpile at the edge of the board—dead pawns, rooks, and knights. It fluttered down off the table, and I reached across to put it back where it had been. He never looked up.

I had closed the door to my room and piled a few chess books in front of it: *My System,* by Aaron Nimzovitch, *Bobby Fischer's Best Games,* the massive *Modern Chess Openings (MCO),* and the last twenty-four issues of *Chess Life,* bound. Overkill: MCO alone, I figured, should be enough to secure the door against my brat sister Abby, but I wanted to make sure that there were no distractions, no escape for G.

97

CHAMPION

G. was an excellent player, nearly as good as I was, but not so imaginative, I think. He never surprised me. On the other hand, it must have amazed him that I, a mere twelve-year-old, beat him every time. The reason I invited him into my room at all was that I needed the practice: I had a big tournament coming up at school, and my first game would be against Robert Schanz.

I'd never played Robert. I'd never even seen him play—he was new to our school, from Utah, I think, or South Dakota, or the moon—nobody knew. He didn't waste his energy on making friends; every ounce of attention went into his chess game. Robert Schanz was like me—a loner.

I'd watched him studying his chess openings. He never ate with the other kids, and he never hung out in the playground. He sat alone in the library going over and over his chess openings. I would linger at the doorway on my way to the lunchroom: I was fascinated by his fingers. They seemed to me like ten slugs sliming down the domes at the tops of the pawns and leaving wet trails across the pages of his MCO. Once Mr. Mose, the librarian, dropped a stack of books right behind Robert Schanz, and he never so much as twittered a brow. I knew I'd have to be in top form for our contest. That's why I sparred with G.

"Jackie, are you dressed? The school bus gonna be here." Bubbe Sophie's Yinglish.

I didn't have to get dressed. I had never un-

98

·CHAMPION·

dressed. I'd been up all night memorizing killer moves from the latest *Chess Life*. Then the game with G.

"I'll be right out, Bubbe."

Sometimes I liked to stare my opponent down. I took a long slow sip of my cold Glass Tea—the Glass Tea I'd been nursing all night long in order to make G. nervous. Then I reached across the board and nudged G.'s chin. I tilted back his large round head until his eyes met mine. G.'s eyes were perfect circles of cerulean blue, the exact blue of my favorite Crayola. He had the look of a vanquished soul. I took hold of his cuff and helped him push his knight forward to escape my rabbi: the only move that wouldn't lose at once. I smiled slowly—but I wasn't sure that I had gotten it quite right. So I went to the mirror over my chest of drawers, pushed aside the piles of chess magazines, and smiled again.

Not quite mean enough. I added a little nod and an evil twist at one corner of my lips. Yes! It was the kind of a slow smile that could curdle borscht at a distance of twenty yards. My Dad used to smile that way for a joke when he played chess with me when I was little. Of course, he didn't have a mean bone in him, so when he put on a mean look it just made you laugh. I looked at Mum and Dad's picture in the little gold frame propped up near the mirror. I gave him and Mum my mean look; I glared evilly right into that old photo, their last photo, at the boat

99
·CHAMPION·

house at Conesus Lake, but I felt like it made them laugh, and that almost made me laugh, so I turned the picture around.

I went back to the chess table and smiled slowly—the right way. It devastated G., I could tell, just as it would devastate Robert Schanz. G. was too proud to let on, of course. He just kept peering back at me with that vacant look.

I moved in my queen. I plunked it down right in front of his *schlemazel* of a king. Just then the door shoved open, Abby stomped in, and G.'s head fell off his shoulders. It hit the floor and rolled across the room to Abby's feet. Abby stuck her fist inside G.'s neck and slung his head under the table.

"Hiya, Golem," she said.

Used to be that Golem terrified her. It had been on Purim when I first made the head we called Golem: paper and paste over a balloon. I'd put the thing on, snuck out, and came knocking on our own door—"Happy Purim!" Abby came to answer, but when she saw me, with my huge round head and piercing eyes of cerulean blue—G's head, G.'s eyes— she ran away crying. Of course, Abby had only been seven then. Now she was eight.

Yes, eight. Very grown-up.

Not.

She wagged her finger at me. "Bubbe says get ready—phew, it's stuffy in here." She made a face. "Must be what's-her-name—the chess spirit."

"Caissa. Very funny. Hey, look what you did to

my books." *Modern Chess Openings* had flopped open, and the back cover was wedged under the door. The other volumes were strewn across the floor.

"I don't know why you read them, Jackie. You never remember anything in them."

"What are you talking about?"

"You've been on the same page for a week."

"I'm very thorough, is all."

"Hmm."

Abby bellied up to the chess table and started toying with the captured pieces. Typical eight-year-old. Her two rag dolls, Moriarty and Hepsybah, dangled from her left hand. Bubbe had spooled her hair into little Shirley Temple curls, and now Abby was sure that she was the cutest, most irresistible kid east of the Mississippi.

In a pig's eye.

"Leave those alone, Abby."

She screwed up her eyes at the chessboard. "Checkmate next move, huh?"

You could say I was surprised. "What do you know about it? You probably don't even know the right way to set the board up."

Abby flounced over to G's side of the chessboard. "Better luck next time, Jack."

"Huh?"

"Funny, you'd think it would be a draw, since

101

it's really just you against you. You could still offer yourself a draw, Jack, and then walk to the other side of the board and agree to it." She put her cheek on the table and looked across the board sideways through the forest of pawns, knights, rabbis, and rooks. "But I guess Golem's too good for you."

Bubbe Sophie called again from the next room. Hurry up, she said.

"What are you talking about, Abby?" I pulled my jacket off the back of Golem's chair where it had been serving as his body. Its limp sleeves had been his arms, but now my arms went in them.

"I just said, it's checkmate next move."

"Two moves, actually." I zipped my jacket. "He's finished."

"No, no, it's you who gets checkmated. On f2, the black square in front and to the right of your king. Because of the shpringer."

"'Shpringer?'"

"That one." She pointed at G.'s knight. "Shpringer guards f2 while the queenie takes the pawn that's on it. Sh'ma!"

"Yeah, and those stupid rag dolls are the king and queen of America."

"They're not stupid. You better say you're sorry." She whispered into her dolls' painted-on ears, "He didn't mean it, Your Majesties." She gave me a dirty look and ran out.

Kids. Checkmate next move, my eye! Golem's head had rolled under his chair. It stared up at me

with that silly grin, a loser's grin. Just to reassure myself, I inspected the position once more. I went over the winning combination in my mind. *Rabbi goes here, rook goes there, and pop goes the weasel—Golem, good night. Shpringer, my eye....*

I froze. I felt my jaw drop and my forehead wrinkle like a crushed juice box. I had overlooked one line of attack. Abby was right. Sh'ma next move: Golem had me beat.

"Jackie, the bus is coming!"

Suddenly my eyelids felt like a couple of barbells. I wished I had time for a hot Glass Tea and forty winks. I heard the groan of the bus at the Hudson Avenue stop a couple of blocks away. If Golem won, so would Robert Schanz. I had to remove the jinx. I quickly rearranged the pieces to give me the win. The first time didn't work—Golem still had a sh'ma on me—so I tried again. I took off the darn shpringer. I gave myself another rabbi. My position was still a mess.

I looked up. Bubbe was at the door watching. "Jackeleh, why don't you let poor Golem win once in a while?" As always, she was wearing an old housedress, faded blue print against a background that might have been white forty years ago. She looked like one of those brown photographs from the old country, and she always smelled of mothballs, except when she'd been cooking: then she smelled of

chicken fat. She was small and round like a Russian doll, and she even wore one of those old-fashioned kerchiefs in the winter. The wrinkles in her face said: *I've laughed some and I've smiled a lot and I've blown plenty of kisses.*

She clucked her tongue and said, "Look at you. Did you sleep last night? Chess, chess, chess! Better you should have one friend than forty chess books, Jackie, Mr. Alone-In-His-Room-Day-And-Night. One friend. Oy, I worry about you, Jackie! One friend."

She wrinkled her nose, then marched to the window and opened it wide, in spite of the cold. She sighed a Bubbe sigh complete with rolling of the eyes, shaking of the head, and pursing of the lips just after. "Or if at least you gonna study something it's worth studying! You know, Jackie, it's written...."

I tried not to listen. Whenever Bubbe said, "It's written," you knew that you were in for a lecture. Instead, I thought of how I could fix things against Golem—and against Robert Schanz....

"You know, Jackie, it's written that so long as a person studies Torah, Death cannot touch him. Rabbi Lipshitz of Poughkeepsie was about to die, but he read and read it the Bible, by the sunlight and by the candlelight. So great his love of Torah it was, what Death couldn't come near. Only, one morning he heard it a robin's song—Tooleedoo! Teedoo!" Bubbe whistled. "And he looked up in delight, and it comes Death to touch him on the cheek, like this." She touched me on the cheek. "At this touch, black

went white, white went black, day became night, and Rabbi Lipshitz met his Maker."

"This isn't Poughkeepsie," I said.

She laughed. "And *Modern Chess Openings* is not the Bible."

"To me it is."

"Oy. I know."

You hear a bird, black goes white—*bubbe mysehs!* Tales for little children. Why did I ever listen? The only black and white you can be sure of is on a chessboard, I was thinking. I tried rearranging a few more pieces. Maybe I could still fix things before I had to catch the bus. But whatever I did, Golem won. I swept all the pieces to the floor with my sleeve. They clattered down, pummeling Golem's head. Bubbe looked down at the mess. The bus honked. Abby yelled, "Jack!"

I said, "I love chess, Bubbe. Even God must play chess. Maybe He's playing chess with Daddy."

She shook her head. "I don't think so."

"I have to get good at it, Bubbe. I don't ever want to lose. I have to get really good."

She shook her head. "I don't think so." She turned away and mumbled something—I think. I think it was a mumble, but it could have been a sob. You can't always tell with bubbes. Like when you hear a word in the thunder, or in a sneeze—or did you? I thought she mumbled: "Oy—when you play

CHAMPION

with God, you lose." And she went to the mirror where my Mum and Dad's picture was, and she turned it to face out again, and she sighed. I think.

I gave her a kiss and ran out to catch the bus.

"A minoot!" Bubbe came out after me. Our breath steamed in the bright fall air. She had my sock cap in her hands, the one with a pompon on top: she had just mended it. She thrust it onto my head with two hands. She held it there a second.

The bus driver honked.

"Bubbe, I gotta go," I said.

She kissed me on the forehead, then let go. "One friend."

Abby slipped between us. She was waving a little scrap of newsprint. "Tuck it in your shirt. It's for luck against Robert Schanz."

Crazy kid. There were three Hebrew letters on it, *shin, mem, ayin:* Sh'ma. She must have asked Bubbe how to write it.

"And anyway, Jackie, don't worry about Robert Schanz," Abby said. "He's the one who doesn't know the right way to set the board up."

"Huh?"

"His little brother Joey told me. Joey's in my music class."

More *bubbe mysehs.* "Right. Thanks, kiddo." I tousled her hair—she closed her eyes and pressed up against my hand like a grateful puppy. Bubbe let me go.

"I'm going to come and watch, Jack," Abby said.

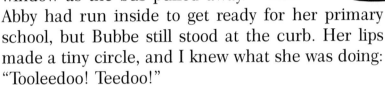

"Bubbe will take me." Bubbe Sophie shrugged.

I tucked the sh'ma under my shirt and climbed into the bus. I guess I was The Human Mezuzah.

I looked out the green-tinted window as the bus pulled away. Abby had run inside to get ready for her primary school, but Bubbe still stood at the curb. Her lips made a tiny circle, and I knew what she was doing: "Tooleedoo! Teedoo!"

I took off my dumb pompon cap, stuffed it into my pocket, and concentrated my mind on defending f2, the deadly black square in front and to the right of my king.

My rabbi moves to the fourth rank. Golem pushes a pawn. I swing my rook over to the open file, and he has to defend with the knight....

The bus was as noisy as a pot of boiling, spattering soup, but if I didn't find a way out of the fix with Golem, I knew my game with Robert Schanz was jinxed. I had to concentrate. I never really talked to anybody anyway; your general school kid had no appreciation of chess, which of course, is what I lived for. They just wouldn't understand.

I squinted at the back of the seat in front of me until it looked like a grid of light and dark squares. In my mind, I numbered the rows 1 to 8 going up the board, and A to H across—just as they did in MCO.

There was a1, the white square down in the left

corner, with my rook on it. There was e8 with Golem's king. There were the queens, his and mine, each on a square of its own color: white queen on white, black king on black.

His queen comes out of nowhere and takes my pawn on the black square f2, right next to my king. Sh'ma! *Why hadn't I seen that?*

"Shumah yourself!" Someone gave me a little shove from the side.

Didn't realize I was saying that out loud! Ignore the bus. Ignore everything. Got to concentrate. Caissa, the chess spirit, is very jealous. If you want to be a winner, you have to give yourself to her with all your heart and all your mind and all your soul. Visualize the position. That darn dark f2 square is the problem, right next to my king. What if I swing out my knight and block it...?

Never mind the rattle of the doors and the groan of the air brakes. Never mind the jabbering cawing hee-hawing kids.

What if I let Golem take the rabbi and then....

"I said, are you ready for the big game?" The chessboard turned into a ripped graffiti-strewn bus seat; beside me, a head taller than me, hair red as a burning bush, wiry, with a goat's narrow chin and bony hands, finger joints the size of marbles—sat Robert Schanz. "What're you, deaf or something?"

"Huh? What are you doing on this bus? You don't take this bus."

"I slept over at my cousin's house. He's nine-

teen, you know. He's on his college chess team. We were booking up on the Scheveningen Sicilian Defense. You good at the Scheveningen Sicilian Defense, Jack?" That grin— that mean grin, *my* mean grin: Robert Schanz had it down.

"Sure. Scheveningen Sicilian Defense. No sweat."

"Great. Should be a good game, then." That grin again. He slapped his bony hand against the back of the seat in front of me, right where my queenside advance was going to skewer Golem's king, I hoped, and he pushed off into the aisle— laughing. I couldn't see the board anymore. Or my pawns. Or the king.

Or anything.

What on earth was the Scheveningen Sicilian Defense?

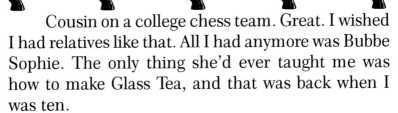

Cousin on a college chess team. Great. I wished I had relatives like that. All I had anymore was Bubbe Sophie. The only thing she'd ever taught me was how to make Glass Tea, and that was back when I was ten.

Here's her recipe, just the way she taught it to me, in case it's some consolation to you when you find yourself on the wrong side of a Scheveningen.

BUBBE SOPHIE'S GLASS TEA

Take it some water—the cold, the hot, I don't care from it. Into a tippot put it, big like your sister Abby's head but only until she is seven. Maybe better you should use it a saucepan; the hole is bigger. Don't make a mess, I'll gonna swing you around my head like a chicken.

Put op the fire—careful how you don't touch— and wait until it comes the big bobbles. The big bobbles I'm talking, not here a bobble, there a bobble.

In a gless put it a tibbeg, could be a Salada, could be a Lipton, I don't care from it.

Into the gless pour the water what you got bobbling on the fire. If you make a mess, as God is my witness, I'll gonna stuff horseradish in your poopik. Swish it a little bit the tibbeg. Take out and put it someplace you shouldn't get it dirty, you could always use it again, you know what I'm talking?

Between your teeth put it a sugar cube—a domino is okay. Pick it op the gless tea, and through the sugar cube, trink. This is a fine gless tea what I told you, and this goes for your whole life.

110

·CHAMPION·

Glass Tea is actually pretty good stuff. It settles your heart, sort of, especially when Bubbe sits next to you, just the two of you alone in the kitchen with those steaming glasses of tea. Abby's asleep. The house feels so empty. You've been orphaned by the rain, by a slippery road on Route 2 back from Conesus Lake. Or maybe it was a bird song, and Dad turned to look off the road for a second....

It's hard for a while, yes, but Abby has Mory and Hepsy, the little squirt, and you, you have chess— and Glass Tea. Bubbe "trinks" through her sugar cube while you "trink" through yours. It makes a funny sound, like a dentist's suction, and it's sweet.

Thank you, Bubbe. I love Glass Tea. But against a Scheveningen, forget it.

Abby's sh'ma crinkled against my belly. Through math and science and social studies all I could think of was pawns and knights. I had almost figured out a way of fixing Golem, when the teacher called on me.

"Jack, Jack, earth to Jack."

"Pawn takes rook," I said. Everyone laughed. My cheeks burned. "Sorry, Mrs. Todd. What was the question?"

But Mrs. Todd didn't get a chance to repeat the question. Robert Schanz stopped laughing long

enough to shout out the answer, which happened to be, "Archduke Ferdinand."

"Very good, Robert!"

He flashed me that smile, and I thought he mouthed the word, Scheveningen....

During lunch I scooted into the school library to look up "Scheveningen." I even got there before Robert. Wished I had my MCO with me. Stacks had been moved and tables shifted to one side in preparation for the tournament. Already, four or five chessboards had been set up, and there was a portable blackboard where the scores would be posted game by game, showing who went on to the next round. It was to be a sudden death Swiss-style tournament: lose one game, and you were out. Even a draw would eliminate you.

Turns out, Schevenigen is a city in the Netherlands, thank you very much. The Encyclopedia Britannica had nothing more to say on the matter, and the Americana was entirely silent. I could only hope that Robert Schanz got the white pieces and had to move first. That way he couldn't play his Scheveningen, which, being a "Defense," had to be for the black side, I figured, the side that always moves second.

One and a half hours to T-time—and I don't mean Glass T. I hadn't eaten anything, and I was starting to feel sleepy. Gotta keep up my concentration. Never mind Golem. Don't be superstitious. If Golem won, it was still me winning, really. Babyish

to think otherwise. That was just a game in the mind. The tournament game, on the other hand....

I kissed two fingers, sneaked them inside my shirt, and touched Abby's sh'ma. The Human Mezuzah. Concentrate on those killer moves from *Chess Life*, Jack, I told myself. I went over them line by line in my mind, the best way I could. Truth is, Abby was right: I have a memory like a sewer grate.

Papers passed through my hands. Voices floated on the air like faraway laughter you hear at the beach. I opened a book, turned pages, closed it, raised my hand, lowered my hand, wrote something with a pencil.

I don't know how much time passed between each thing and the next. At one point I stood in line for something. At another point, I was putting things back inside my desk. I just concentrated on ranks and diagonals and files, light squares, dark squares, killer moves. I touched my belly and felt Abby's sh'ma. The Human Mezuzah vs. The Amazing Mr. Slug Fingers.

The bell rang, and the classroom emptied—that much I remember. I must have walked down the hallway to the school library then, although I don't remember any walking, because the next thing I knew I was seated at a chessboard across from Robert Schanz—and I had the white pieces.

"You gonna move or what?"

I swallowed hard and pushed my king pawn two squares forward into the center. I could only pray that I wasn't waltzing into a Scheveningen.

Schanz fingered his king's pawn. He lingered over it maddeningly, then did the same thing I had done: he pushed it two squares. Normally I would attack at once by jumping my knight out on the kingside—that's what they did in the *Chess Life*—but what if that was just what Robert was waiting for? What if that was the very move that the chess mavens had plotted against in Scheveningen? I decided to do something different. I pushed a pawn on the other side, making a little hole where I could post my rabbi later on. I yawned. I rubbed my eyes.

He slammed down his rabbi, aiming straight at my f2. No sweat: my king defended that square. As long as the black pieces didn't gang up on it, I was okay. I sneaked my rabbi into the little hole I had made for it. If Schanz didn't defend his center pawn it would be a goner. Had they thought of that in Scheveningen? Now Robert Schanz placed his elbows on the table and rested his chin on the heels of his hands, deep in thought.

Apparently they hadn't. Score one for the home team.

I yawned again. Schanz stirred uncomfortably but never looked up.

I shouldn't have let on how tired I was; it might give him a psychological advantage. I thought it would be a good moment to try out my evil grin, but I felt

so sleepy, I could barely find my dimples. Robert Schanz was a white globe with cerulean blue eyes—*no, that's Golem! Wake up!* I shook the sawdust out of my head. I stared at the board. *Concentrate! Remember Bubbe's story: if a robin sings, don't listen.*

Do you think there really is a chess spirit called Caissa who hovers nearby whenever people play chess? I could have sworn I felt a slight breeze from the beating of her wings. I thought I felt the glint of her golden body like sunlight in my eyelashes. Just then I smelled mothballs—had Caissa been in storage? I looked up. Bubbe Sophie had walked into the library with Abby at her side dragging along Moriarty and Hepsybah.

I should not have looked up. I remembered Rabbi Hoozit's bird song, the one that let Death in. Did Death smell like mothballs? Abby winked and waved, but Bubbe Sophie was grim. She stared at the chessboard with the intensity of a Robert Schanz. She cocked her head at it this way and that. Bubbe could be totally weird sometimes. I just hoped she wouldn't embarrass me in front of the school kids.

All at once, I thought I heard a clap of thunder. I looked down at the board again. The Amazing Mr. Slug Fingers had squeezed his queen out through the narrow passage in front of his king and smashed it down on the rim of the board. It was drooling over

my center pawn, ready to snap it up on his very next move. Tit for tat. Those Scheveningen fellows must have been pretty sharp. I wasn't fool enough to look up again, but I was aware that a crowd was gathering around our table. I hadn't realized what a long time Robert and I had been taking; all the others had finished their games already. We were the main event now. Which of us would make it to Round Two?

I couldn't help it: I yawned again. *Concentrate!* I had to do something about the threat to my center pawn. I fixed my eyes on it.

Should I move out my shpringer, I mean, my knight, or push up another pawn to protect it? Or should I take his pawn and let him take mine? Maybe I should just ignore his queenie, I mean, his queen, and do something else entirely, something the Scheveningen-ers never expected.

Scheveningen-ers. Scheveningen-INGEN-ers. Scheveningen-ingen-INGEN-ers. Scheveningen-ingen-ingen-INGEN-ers. Tooleedoo! Teedoo! My eyes closed. I smelled moth balls. I smelled Glass Tea. I tasted the sugar cube between my teeth. Someone was touching my cheek....

I shook myself awake, I yawned again, and, just like that, I moved the knight.

Isn't it the truth? You study and you study, you cover your ears and tunnel your eyes, and then, when the moment comes—you just move. My knight came down like thunder—not because I was trying to scare

116

CHAMPION

anybody, but because I had just shaken myself awake and my hand was a little unsteady. The table quaked The crowd inched back. Robert Schanz trembled.

I was kind of enjoying these effects when I noticed something that made my blood run cold: at the same time that Robert's queen threatened my center pawn, it was taking aim at a second target, which I hadn't noticed before: my f2 pawn! Just like Golem. My knight move had defended the center pawn okay, but all Robert had to do was move in his queen, capture at f2—his rabbi backed it up—and...sh'ma!

Worse—I could hardly believe my eyes: f2 was white! The black f2 square had turned white. I looked at my queen, my white queen, and sure enough, the square it rested on was black. My white left corner square, a1, was black as well.

White had turned to black and black to white. I didn't dare look out the window to see what had become of day and night. Tooleedoo! Teedoo!

Caissa, why did you do this to me? Haven't I loved you enough? How could you leave me like this in the middle of everything, with a hopeless position? How could you let me neglect my f2? All I've got left is this note on my belly and, maybe later, some of Bubbe's Glass Tea—loser's tea. Tooleedoo! Teedoo!

Now I knew who Robert Schanz was—Death.

·CHAMPION·

He reached his hand across the board. I turned my cheek just a little bit, ready for him to take me....

Instead, he turned up his palm and shrugged. "Draw?"

"Huh?"

"Do you want to agree to a draw?"

I stopped shivering. I closed my mouth. I noticed that I was still alive. Alive? I wasn't even checkmated. "A draw? A tie? Even-Steven? After only four moves?"

"Yeah. Ya wanna or not?"

I took his hand. We shook. He smiled. I tried to hide my surprise that his fingers weren't slimy after all.

"Good game," he said. "I guess this means neither one of us gets into the next round, though."

"I guess."

Around us people were clucking their tongues, shaking their heads, and settling down to play their Round Two games, which had been held up for Robert and me. Abby was among the head shakers.

"What is it?" I said, and Abby started to say something, but Bubbe cut her off:

"Why don't you two boyehs come home and have it a nice gless tea, maybe a macaroon?"

Robert folded his chessboard and dozed the pieces into a satchel. "Sounds good to me."

Abby tried to stop him. "Wait!"

But again Bubbe cut her off. "Come, Abby, others need chess table. You can have a macaroon. Come."

"Bubbe," I whispered. "I heard the robin."

"You what?" She said.

"Black went white," I said.

And Bubbe said, *"Bubbe mysehs!"*

It was good Glass Tea. You should have seen Robert Schanz work on those sugar cubes: they lasted about two sips each before he had to get another. Not a bad system; the sugar is the best part. We had a few laughs over Glass Tea.

"That Scheveningen," I said, "you really had me with that Scheveningen. Why did you let me off with a draw?"

"Well, it wasn't really a Scheveningen," he said, looping another sugar. "If you wanna know the truth, I don't really know what a Scheveningen is."

"What do you mean, you don't know what a Scheveningen is? I watched you reading chess books all week in the library."

"My cousin gave me his MCQ...."

"MCO," I said.

"Whatever. I look at the diagrams. I push around the pieces. I can't really follow that stuff, but it's something to do at lunchtime. I don't know anybody at school."

"You know me. You can sit with me at lunch."

"Hey!" Abby plunked Moriarty and Hepsybah down on the white enamel kitchen table and looked

·CHAMPION·

straight at Robert. "You still didn't tell him why you gave him a draw when you were about to checkmate him—or do you want me to?"

"Oh, that. Well, I set up the board wrong." Another sugar.

"Huh?"

Robert looked down. "I set it up all sideways. The wrong color square was in the left corner; that makes all the other squares the wrong color. I only caught it after my last move. Rule is, you have to start all over, right?" Abby nodded. "And I didn't think I could get so far in a second game with you, so I wanted to get the draw before you noticed the mixed-up colors. Sorry! I saw you yawning. I figured you were bored with the way I played, that you were just kind of toying with me. I'm really pretty lousy at chess."

That's why my f2 had been white and why my white queen had stood on a black square!

"No, no," I said to Robert Schanz, "I was just yawning because I was tired!"

Robert Schanz hit his forehead with the heel of his hand. "You were scared of my Scheveningen, and I was scared of your yawn." He began to laugh.

Tired as I was, I couldn't help laughing along. I got Glass Tea up my nose, and that made us laugh even harder.

Finally, I just had to close my eyes. I folded my arms on the table before me and rested my head on them, just for a second.

It was a long second. When I opened my eyes, Bubbe was tucking me in bed. She had cleaned up my room. All my chess books were back on the shelf. Abby's sh'ma was on the night table next to my bed. The pieces were on the chessboard ready to go, and Golem's head sat on the post of his chair, right over my jacket, which Bubbe had slung over the back, the same way I always did. Abby was nestled in the chair across from Golem, fast asleep with Moriarty and Hepsybah in her lap. I could see she had made a pretty good opening, and Golem was going to be in big trouble when she woke up.

"Where's Robert?" I said.

"He had to go home. Nice boy. You'll see him tomorrow. You'll play chess, yah? Maybe a Scheveningen. Maybe a nice Gless Tea."

I drifted off to sleep while Bubbe stroked my hair and mumbled—or did she? She might have been just clearing her throat, or I could have been asleep and dreaming, but I thought she said: "Maybe could be I was wrong, Jackie. Maybe God does play chess with your Daddy. Maybe He offers him a draw, even, like Robert Schanz. Yah, could be it's a draw. Mummy too!" Next either she yawned or she said (I'm not sure which): "Because maybe God set the board up funny." And she laughed, and she laughed, and she kissed me on the forehead.

Bubbes.

Well, I confess I don't know if Daddy has made it to the next round in the Swiss Tournament in the Garden of Eden—or Mummy. Maybe it's not so important down here, after all. A person has to move on, and there are plenty of folks to love or to be friends with, even if the board is set up funny.

Robert Schanz and I shared plenty of Glass Tea after that. Neither of us ever figured out the Scheveningen, even though Abby found it in the MCO and tried and tried to teach us. We kind of lost interest in chess eventually. I mean we stopped studying it and just played for fun. We found a lot of other people to play with, too. Robert started to say, "sh'ma" for "checkmate" just the way I did, and he called the bishops "rabbis." Both of us, for fun, called the knights "shpringers," the way Abby did. Turns out, it's the German word for knight—the little smarty! Maybe Bubbe taught her.

Guess what? It caught on. Next tournament— in which I actually made it to Round Two before getting whacked on my f2—everybody was shouting "Sh'ma!" and talking about "rabbis" and "shpringers." For the first time in my life, I was actually in fashion—I even talked to people on the bus.

So when I heard that robin and got touched on the cheek, I suppose it was the death of my life as a loner and not the death of me. Now I have forty books—and a friend.

THE ALL-STAR SUPER KLUTZ

BY TONI LYNN DOVE

Toni Lynn Dove

I was inspired to write All-Star Super Klutz because I love baseball! I played with my family every Sunday when the weather allowed, but I wasn't all that great. My brothers, however, were awesome players who stayed in Little League for years, and my sister was the only girl on the league! I was content being their number one fan.

I live in North Carolina with my nine month old son, Sky, where I draw children's' portraits, and write every chance I get. I plan to have Sky running bases soon, but he has to learn to walk first!

THE ALL-STAR SUPER KLUTZ

There are times when life gets your attention by hitting you where it hurts. Newton got clonked on the head by an apple and wrote the law of gravity. Franklin's kite was struck by lightning, and he discovered electricity. And Goldman got a bloody nose and discovered baseball.

Goldman's me, by the way. You can call me Jody unless you're one of those military types who like to call people by their last name.

A lot of people might think that getting hit by a stray foul ball would be the surest way to make someone really hate baseball. For me, it was love at first bruise.

Bruises are a part of my life, so I don't hold anything against them. I've gotten all kinds; shin bruises from falling down the stairs, toe bruises from walking barefoot into tree stumps, elbow bruises from bumping into everything in sight, knee bruises, shoulder bruises...I've even had finger bruises.

In case you're wondering what in the world is wrong with me, I'll tell you right now. I am a klutz. I can't help it. My father is a klutz and his father before him was a klutz. It's in the family genes.

Mom says I've just hit a growth spurt, I'm all knees and elbows, and I'll grow out of it in time. I

have grown a lot lately. But just when I think Mom may be right, and I might not be doomed to being forever a klutz, I do something like bumping my head on the car door twice in a row.

So maybe you see why I wasn't so surprised to be introduced into "America's Favorite Pastime" with a bang. Literally.

I was on my way home from school when it happened. It was Friday, and I was in a hurry, so I'd have a chance to play and get dirty before dark. My Mom is the type who can find a speck of dirt on a beach. She's especially crazy about being clean when it comes to the Shabbat.

"You want God to see you looking like something from a dumpster?"

I always want to say. "What? God doesn't see me all the time?" But trust me, the day I do that is the day you will never see or hear of Jody Goldman again!

Anyway, I was just passing by the park, where some kids were throwing a ball around. I wasn't paying much attention. I had never really thought about sports much up till then. I mean, when a guy plays kickball and everyone covers their head and cringes, even the guy's own team, that guy gets the hint real quick that sports aren't for him!

All of a sudden I heard someone yell.

"Heads up!"

So of course I lifted my head up....

And got belted in the face.

The baseball cracked on my nose with a sickening thud and rolled to my feet.

"You okay, kid?"

"Throw that ball will ya?"

I was so mad that I picked the ball up and threw it as hard as I could at the guy who asked me to. To my surprise, he caught it. Then he took his glove off and waved his hand in front of him like it hurt.

"Ow, kid. You got some arm on you."

When he held out his sore hand, I noticed it was a bit red on the palms. "My name is Thomas, Thomas Ringer. Do you play ball?"

Talking with a bloody nose isn't easy, and neither is shaking hands but I managed to do both.

"I don't play sports." I said, though with me holding my nose and all, it sounded more like I was saying "I dode pay spords."

Thomas whistled. "I can't believe it! You don't play sports!" he said, "Man, if you get control of that fastball of yours, you could be the best pitcher in Little League!"

"The best what?" I asked. It sounded like he said picture, but I knew I had to be mixed up. "A picture of what?"

Thomas shook his head like I was crazy. "How old are you?"

"Twelve." I said.

"You are twelve years old and don't know what a pitcher is?"

Thomas couldn't believe it. I couldn't blame him. Later on I found out that baseball ran in his blood just like klutz ran in mine. His dad was tossing him stuffed baseballs as a baby, for goodness sake!

After I cleaned my nose with my T-shirt, Thomas decided to show me what I'd been missing. He got frustrated a few times. Like when I tried to wear a baseball mitt upside-down or ran toward my house when he yelled "Run Home!"

The funny thing was, I didn't mind messing up for once. As soon as I got the basics down, I discovered I could handle almost anything baseball had to offer.

I could throw hard, catch just about anything that came at me, and even hit okay if someone threw it easy enough and straight down the middle. Best of all, I didn't knock anyone down, bump my head, or trip over my own feet even once!

My best skill, by far, was pitching. Somehow, I just naturally knew how to slide the ball into the strike zone. And I threw it FAST!

I found out just how fast when an hour later, a few other kids drifted over, and we formed a game. I struck out the first three guys who came to bat. Even Thomas, who was the home run king of the field according to the other guys, had a hard time hitting my fastball!

I got so caught up in the game that I didn't pay attention to the time.

Then one of the guys said he had to go home

CHAMPION

for supper and I noticed the time REAL quick. If I wasn't home before dark, there was gonna be trouble!

"I have to go!" I said.

Thomas wrote his phone number on the inside of a bubble gum wrapper. "My dad coaches a Little League Team. The season starts soon. See if your Mom and Dad will sign you up!"

I said good-bye to everyone, and I was on my way. I was so caught up in thinking about baseball that I forgot everything else. When I opened the front door, Mom was standing there waiting. The smell of food was wafting all through the house. When I saw candles lit in the background, I knew for sure that I was in for it!

"Where have you been? And what have you done to your shirt? You're a mess! A mess! And I just lit candles for Shabbat! Get upstairs and into clean clothes. Pronto!"

She didn't mention my nose. My family is so used to me coming home with some injury or the other that they don't even ask about them anymore.

I wanted to tell someone about my new love for baseball and how incredibly GOOD I was, but I wasn't desperate enough to face down Mom in dirty clothes. I went upstairs, washed fast, and changed into a clean outfit.

I had just managed to stuff all of my dirty clothes between my mattresses in a way that wasn't too lumpy

and noticeable, when Dad came in to inspect me.

"Your mother sent me in to see if you were planning to join us tonight." Dad smiled, with more than a hint of sarcasm. "You look sharp, Son! That's good because we have company over tonight!

"Sam Fielding and his family have been working with the firm for a few months now, and your mom figured it was about time we were sociable.

"One word of advice before I go back downstairs, Son.... Don't give your Mom any problems. You know how she gets with company coming."

I knew all right. When Dad turned to leave, I decided that I could put my dirty clothes in the hamper, after all.

I was a little disappointed that we had company. I always kind of liked when it was just Mom, Dad, Shelly (my nauseating big sister), and me during Shabbat. After dinner, the whole family would go to the living room to sit. No TV, no computers...in other words, nothing but talking. And boy did I have something to talk about tonight!

I was always embarrassed around people I didn't know well. And for some reason I turned into Super Klutz when people were watching.

To make matters worse, the Fieldings had a daughter my age. Joanna Fielding! We weren't in any of the same classes, so I'd never really got to know her beyond seeing her at the company picnic and in the halls at school. She was definitely pretty though, at least from far away.

Dad had said I looked sharp, but I ran to the mirror over my dresser to give myself a once-over anyway. Bad idea. My nose was blue and swollen and a bruise was starting under my left eye.

At least I'd gone to the barber recently, though, so my hair wasn't poofing out all around my kippah. I sighed and ran downstairs.

Mom was finishing dinner. Shelly (who didn't have one iota of the klutz gene in her) was looking perfect, as usual, and giving Mom a hand with the food.

Mom and Shelly were talking non-stop about Shelly's new boyfriend, Kevin. I was waiting for a good opportunity to ask about Little League. When Shelly mentioned that Kevin was a pitcher for the high school team, I saw my chance and took it.

"Guess what, Mom?" I said, "I've decided to be a baseball player."

Shelly laughed. "Don't be silly, Jody. You've never played baseball a day in your life. Kevin is a great baseball player, and he's played since he was four years old. Of course, he was playing at T-ball then, but that's just the point. You have to work hard and long to be any good."

"I know that." I said. I turned to mom. "I met a boy at the park today. His Dad's a baseball coach, and he wants me to be on his team!"

Shelly laughed again.

"You do realize that everyone will be watching you, don't you? How do you expect to run the bases when you can't even keep from tripping over your own feet? The whole thing will be a BIG embarrassment, and not just for you. You're my brother you know. When you mess up, it reflects on me.

"Why don't you stick to what you know you're good at? With all that falling and slipping you'd be a shoo-in for Clown College!"

I sighed. It was just my luck that Kevin played baseball. Shelly would have just ignored baseball and me normally, but if she had a boyfriend involved, I was in for it!

I was just getting ready to say something to get her back for the Clown College bit, when Mom nudged past me with a stack of plates and napkins.

"Shelly, that's enough of that! I've always told you kids you can do anything you put your mind to, and I stand by my word."

Then Mom turned to me and winked.

"Now, Mr. All-Star, if it isn't too much trouble, why don't you pitch a few plates and forks on the table and prepare to take a break between seasons. It'll be dark soon, and I think I hear our company at the door. We'll talk about getting you involved in a team later."

I made a face at Shelly. She just huffed and walked out of the room. Mom could be cool when she wanted to. I smiled and finished setting the table.

That night, I never got around to talking about

baseball again. Something about Joanna made me feel shy. She was even prettier than I'd realized. She had big dark eyes and shiny hair that she wore short.

She seemed just as shy as me. Our parents kept trying to get us to talk to each other. They asked me about school and asked her if we had any classes together. We mumbled answers quickly and smiled politely, then went back to paying attention to our feet.

Mom sent me to the kitchen for challah that she had been keeping warm. That's when the catastrophe of the night happened. I carried a basket loaded up with challah from the kitchen with no problem. Then I walked to the table to place the basket before Dad and tripped over the leg of a chair.

You can imagine what happened next. The wine bottle tipped over and wine spilled on the nice white tablecloth, as the challah landed in Joanna's lap! My face turned bright red. I helped clean up and rushed to my room.

I sat on my bed and thought about baseball. I imagined Joanna sitting in the stands watching me play. Boy, would she get a laugh! Knowing me, I'd trip over first base and clonk the catcher on his head with my bat!

I was starting to think there might be something to what Shelly had said. I mean, it wasn't like I had played baseball for long. Did I really want to

CHAMPION

make a fool of myself in front of a crowd of people? On the other hand, I really liked baseball. I just didn't know what to do.

I cleaned up and changed my shirt, dreading the walk back down the stairs. I put it off as long as I could, then took a deep breath and made my way back to the dining room.

The room always looked beautiful with just the dim lights overhead and the soft candlelight. I was especially glad because it was harder to see how red my face was!

Mom sat in her place near Dad. He waited for her to get settled and nodded for me to sit.

Suddenly nothing mattered but that moment, with Dad's deep, singsong voice making kiddush and the feeling of warmth and family around me. The smell of dinner hung heavy and spicy in the air and the candlelight danced on the windows. I sneaked a look at Joanna. Her eyes were closed and a small smile was on her lips. This was something we had in common, hearing those same words every week from childhood. I sighed and sank back into the chair.

Everyone had finished eating and was relaxing in the living room. Dad had the Torah spread open on the living room table. He looked up expectantly when I walked in.

Shelly grinned at me and Joanna looked anywhere but at me. I could feel my face going hot. I sat in a chair as far from Joanna and her parents as possible, then looked at my feet like they were the

most interesting things in the world.

When Dad found what he was looking in the Torah, we all sat quietly for a moment. Then Dad lifted the Torah and began to read a passage he'd chosen the night before.

"Hear, O Israel, you are coming near to the battle against your enemies; let your heart not be faint; do not be afraid, do not panic, and do not be broken before them. For the Lord your God is the One Who goes with you, to fight for you with your enemies to save you." *(Deuteronomy 20:3-4)*

Dad said he felt that this verse was saying that when you let God be your champion then you were the champion also. "With God by your shoulder you can endure."

Later that night, I lay in bed thinking over the verse Dad had read.

I knew that baseball wasn't a battle really, and maybe the other teams weren't exactly enemies, but for some reason that verse really spoke to me. I was always afraid to try new things and baseball was something big for me because people would be looking at me.

But knowing that I was never alone, that God was with me, made me feel like I could do anything! I decided I would play baseball! And if I messed up, so what? I'd just work harder to do better! I would ENDURE!

Mom was true to her word, and in a few weeks time, she'd signed me up with Thomas's team, the Tigers. Thomas embarrassed me by telling everyone that I was the best pitcher he'd ever seen.

"You guys just watch! Jody will be the next Nolan Ryan in no time!"

And there I was, with no idea what he was talking about. I was so embarrassed I looked at my feet. It seemed like I was doing a lot of that lately!

Coach Ringer finally made Thomas quiet down, tossed me a ball and mitt, and told me to show him what I could do.

I pitched a couple of fastballs over the plate and Coach nodded appreciatively.

"You've got to have more than a fastball, though, Jody. A good pitcher can lose his arm quickly throwing nothing but heaters. Let's see how you do with a curve ball. We want you to endure as far into the game as possible."

There was that word again. Endure.

Without too much work I was soon throwing all sorts of pitches.

"You've got to work on your hitting though," Coach said as I lobbed my third pop fly straight to center field or cut my bat through thin air. "We can put in pinch hitters for our pitchers, but I like everyone to come to bat at least once a game."

"You are so good, Jody. I wish I could pitch like that!" Thomas said after practice.

"Yeah, but I can't hit like you, and you heard

your dad, we all have to hit once a game. At least you don't have to pitch!" I was definitely starting to worry. I'd counted on doing what I was good at and nothing else.

"Yeah, well that's Dad. He wants everyone to have a turn. All coaches aren't like that, you know. Some care way more about winning than anything else."

Thomas looked proud when he said this, and I couldn't argue with him. It was cool of Coach to let everyone play no matter what, but I was still nervous about it.

When I got home that night, I told Dad I needed help. We made a date to go to the park after school where he could throw a few balls to me, or maybe I should say at me!

I learned fast that I hadn't inherited my baseball skills from Dad! He either pitched the ball way over my head, about three feet to my left, or straight into my stomach. After a few practices with Dad, I decided to save my allowance and stick to the batting cage at Fun Place.

Dad seemed relieved, and promised to match my savings so I'd get more hitting time. He was happy to watch me hit from the other side of a fence, and he cheered every time the bat came in contact with the ball, whether it was a foul that flew over the back of my head or a hard grounder to third base.

One night, I'd just finished my homework when I heard a tap on the door. Dad came in holding a

box.

"I bought this for you. A guy at the store helped me pick it out."

I was so excited that I ripped open the box. Inside was a brand new mitt. It was a golden honey color. I held it to my face and breathed in the scent of oil and leather.

"Wow! Thanks, Dad! It fits perfectly." I couldn't wait to break it in.

Dad held out a couple of rubber bands and a small bottle of oil. He showed me how to rub the oil into the leather until it was no longer shiny, then bend the glove and strap the rubber bands around it. I was impressed.

"Your mom showed me a few tricks. Seems her Dad was into baseball. I've never really been one for sports, you know." Dad looked a bit embarrassed. He was probably thinking about all the balls he'd thrown at me.

"You know, Jody," said dad, "I am really proud of you. I know that you've been nervous about playing in front of an audience, but I am glad you are sticking to it."

Dad laughed, remembering something.

"I was just thinking about the first time I walked into a courtroom, I was so nervous that I couldn't tie my tie straight. Then I tripped halfway down the aisle. You know what, though? I got right back up, won my first case, and now I have my own firm.

"It takes endurance, son. God gives us all spe-

cial gifts, but that doesn't mean we don't have to work at using them. You keep on practicing, and no matter what, win or lose, you'll know you did the best with those gifts He's given you."

After that, I worked even harder. Everyday, after I finished my homework, I threw pitches and ran up and down the block.

My pitching just got better and better. I'd even made up my own pitch called the Super Greaser. It was a fastball I threw, split-fingered with just a little bit of spin to it. If I executed it perfectly, the Super Greaser went straight down the middle, got a good hitter's confidence up, then curved inside right before it went over the plate.

Coach said he saw a definite improvement in my hitting and made me a starting pitcher.

Kids at school noticed the change, too. Thomas and I had become really good buddies and he commented on it one day.

"You know, Jody, you used to be this goofy, quiet kid who was always bumping into things." Then he laughed. "You're still goofy and quiet, but you don't bump into things so much anymore!"

I laughed and threw a wadded paper ball at him.

I sometimes passed Joanna in the hall. She was always nice and smiling, but after she'd say hi, she'd go down the hall giggling with her friends.

"Girls!" Thomas said one day when I sat watching Joanna and her crew walking away. "All they do is giggle, giggle, giggle, and talk about shopping! I can't see how you can even talk to them!"

"Oh, yeah?" I said. "What about Shelly?"

Thomas had a huge crush on Shelly. His face turned bright red, and he stalked off to class without answering me.

The weather was getting cooler and *Fall Ball* was starting in earnest. Thomas and I went to the park just about everyday to get in extra practice. Our first game was in a week!

Thomas had a sleep-over for the whole team at his house the weekend before the game. We ate pizza and popcorn then laughed at old scary movies all night.

I had the craziest dream.

I was running the bases in big, red clown shoes, and every time I tried to pass a base it grew tall and tripped me. Everyone in the stands were laughing and eating popcorn. I'd finally made it to home plate when a Frankenstein monster hit me in the face with a piece of pizza. The crowd cheered and started throwing popcorn at me.

I woke up covered in popcorn and sweat. Thomas was laughing at me.

"I had to throw 23 pieces of popcorn at you to wake you up! And you look like you've seen a ghost!"

I threw my pillow at him and went back to sleep.

Finally it was the day of our first game. During

practice, there had always been a few parents watching in the stands. It had taken me a while to get used to them, but at least they were on our side. Tonight there would be people who wanted the Tigers to lose.

I was so nervous that I paced back and forth across the living room until Dad told me to go to my room and wear out my own carpet. I gulped and decided it was time to change for the game anyway.

The uniform was so cool! The thought of putting it on made me feel a little better. The shirts were orange with blue tiger stripes on the sleeves. We got to choose our own numbers, as long as no one else already had them. I chose 20 for the verse Dad had read the night I first knew I wanted to be a ballplayer.

I slipped the shirt over my head. It was made of flexible cotton and, thanks to Mom, smelled like fabric softener. I was really looking forward to staining it up. I hoped I got a chance to slide into second base.

Who was I kidding? I just hoped I got a chance to get on base at all!

Finally, it was time to go. I walked downstairs, and Mom started taking pictures right away. She and Dad looked so proud that, even though my mouth was dry, I tried to smile for every click and flash of the camera.

141

CHAMPION

Even Shelly said I looked like a real baseball player.

"Now let's just see if you play like one. Kevin's coming to the game tonight, you know."

That night we played hard, but so did the Sharks. It was a home game, so we were batting at the bottom of the ninth. We were tied 2-1 and Thomas Ringer was on deck. There was one man left on third and two outs.

Every Tiger was wearing rally caps and shouting, "You can do it! C'mon! Hit it hard!"

The pitcher had a good curve ball but he wasn't all that fast. This time he threw the ball slow and straight down the middle. It was a perfect pitch for a hard hitter like Thomas. He swung hard and hit the ball to left field and toward the fence. The left fielder didn't even try to catch it! He just watched it whiz over his head.

Everyone in the dugout went crazy! The guy on third tagged up and ran for home.

I heard Mom, Shelly, and the rest of the Tigers' crowd screaming from the stands. We'd won our first game!

Thomas jogged around the bases, a big grin on his face. He got halfway to second when a cheer went up from the other team. Their center fielder had run all the way to left field and caught the ball in mid-air!

I felt my heart drop to my stomach.

The two teams lined up to slap hands and say

142

·CHAMPION·

"Good game." "Good game." "Good game."

The Sharks said it with a lot more enthusiasm than we did.

The Tigers met at a pizza place for dinner, but it was hard to enjoy it when the Sharks were sitting a few tables over talking loudly about their victory.

Coach told us we'd played a good game, and we'd just work harder and do better next time.

Shelly took me to the side and said "Kevin said you were the best twelve-year-old pitcher he'd ever seen. He didn't believe me when I told him you'd only been playing a couple of months!"

"You worked hard out there, Son. Remember what I said about enduring and doing the best you can with God's gifts," said Dad. "We're proud of you."

"There'll be other games, Jody," said Mom. "There will be plenty of chances for you to win. Buck up!"

I thought about the verse in the Torah and decided that mom was right. The Tigers would meet the Sharks again someday, and when we did, we were going to win!

The whole team felt the same way, and we worked harder than ever. No one missed a practice if they could help it.

We did win our next game, and the next, and the next. By the end of the season, we were undefeated and so were the Sharks.

It all came down to the last game. It was time to find out who would be going to the playoffs and who would be going home.

Everybody came to watch me play. Dad, Mom, Shelly...even the Fieldings were there. I was disappointed to see that Joanna hadn't showed, but I soon forgot all about it.

The game started out rough and stayed that way. The Sharks were having a good night trying their newest starting pitcher, Joe, who was showing off his skills on a no-hitter.

I wasn't doing so bad myself and by the top of the 9th inning, there were still no points for either side.

Forty-five minutes later, I stood on the mound looking over my shoulder to see how the guy on first was behaving. I felt nervous. Crazy nervous! Up until a hard line drive whizzed close enough by my face to blow me a kiss, I'd matched The Sharks pitch-for-pitch with my own no-hitter.

Now my Super Greaser was down to plain grease and no "super" and I'd let my first man on base. It was a double whammy that the guy who'd ripped that line drive by me was the same guy who still had a no-hitter to his name.

Joe.

Sweat dripped into my eyes and I saw Coach motioning for Jonnie Hulbert to warm-up. "Two more outs...just two more. God is on my shoulder. Endurance." I said it over and over in a kind of chant.

144

CHAMPION

Then I closed my eyes, opened them, and concentrated on a change-up.

Jonnie swung and hit an easy pop fly right over the back of his head and into the catcher's mitt. I heard those beautiful words.

"Your'rrrrre OUT!"

My confidence was back, and Joe? Well. His confidence was fading fast. He wasn't so antsy on base, anyway.

In no time I'd struck out the next guy and we were back in the dugout. I was feeling good. Bottom of the ninth and our best guys were lined up to hit.

Sure enough, Shane Williams smacked a strong fly ball to right field that sped past the right fielder's glove and left him confused long enough for Shane to score a double. Then good ol' Buck Lee hit a firm grounder towards third base and made it to first before the ball was in the first baseman's possession and in time to give the crowd a wave.

I was watching and not worrying a bit. The next guy up was Roger Bryan, and he was as steadfast as a rock. He'd get out there and load up the bases just in time for the ol' Home Run King, Thomas Ringer, to bring the boys home!

I leaned back, stretched and smiled.

One out and two strikes later, I wasn't smiling anymore. Bryan had struck out without once touching the ball and Ringer was hitting hard and straight into the foul zone. He'd hit five foul balls already.

This guy, Joe, was good! Now he'd pushed away our best hitters and I was pacing on deck.

I pled with Coach to let in a pinch-hitter but he said that all players had to take the deck at least once a game, and since I'd put it off, it was my turn at bat.

Literally.

Ringer hit yet another foul and the third baseman cradled it in his glove without breaking a sweat.

Suddenly, there I was, Super Klutz Deluxe, balancing a bat on my shoulder and settling into my favorite Chipper Jones stance.

The first ball flew by my elbows before I could blink an eye.

"STEEEEE-RIKE one!"

I actually swung at the second ball and hit nothing but air.

I took the time to stretch my shoulders. I looked over into the stands. Everyone was watching intently. No one made a sound. For a minute I was ready to give up.

The whole game, no, the whole season was on my shoulders! Me! Super Klutz Deluxe, Master of the Banana Peel Slip!

I closed my eyes. "Please, God, give me the strength to win and the grace to lose if it be your will."

I opened my eyes, got into stance, and everything went in slow motion.

Joe was wearing black paint under each eye and he glared at me beneath the brim of his hat. I saw beads of sweat on his upper lip.

Then he leaned back to throw the ball. The ball flew from his fingers with a bit of a spin. I knew it would curve in, so I stepped back.

Wait...Wait...SWING!

I felt the unmistakable and beautiful sound of the bat coming in contact with the ball. Oh that wonderful *clunk!* Is there any more beautiful song to a hitter's ear?

I stood still for a second watching it fly toward center field. The guys on base were biting their lips, tagging up, and just waiting for the perfect chance to run.

Joe looked at the ball like it was a U.F.O. or something.

Suddenly an eerie hush fell over the field. The ball was over the fence. I'd hit my first home run!

When I strolled, third in line, over home plate, I felt like I was going to be hugged and slapped on the back till the end of time. I was in a daze.

Dad patted my back and said one word. "Endurance."

Shelly and Mom just squealed and cried. Thanks to them, I was now in danger of being kissed till the end of time along with everything else!

When we stood in line to say our "good games",

147

CHAMPION

none of us could keep the big, goofy grins off our faces. I was especially looking forward to shaking Joe's hand. I had to admit, the guy was good!

When I finally reached him, I slapped his hand with feeling and said. "You are good, man!"

"Thanks. But I'm not exactly a man."

That's when I realized that "Joe" was "Jo", as in Joanna Fielding!

I couldn't talk for a second. Then I squeaked, "You were awesome!"

"You weren't so bad yourself," she grinned.

My jaw dropped. I didn't remember making the rest of my "good games". All I could think was, "She's beautiful and she plays ball!"

What could be better?

I've had a few no-hitters under my belt since that day, but I've never hit another ball anywhere near the fence.

You know what, though? That's okay. Jo's gonna meet me at Fun Place and give me some pointers on my stance in exchange for helping her with her fast ball.

Practice. Practice. Practice. We'll probably have to go every week!

You know, sometimes enduring isn't all that hard!

GREAT SAVE!

BY DEBBIE SPRING

149
CHAMPION

Debbie Spring

I have been a professional writer since 1985, writing children's plays, novels, short stories and picture books. I have won several awards and short story contests including the 1996 and 1999 Brendon Donnelly Award for excellence in Children's Literature. My stories have been published in Canadian and American journals, anthologies and magazines.

My picture book WILMA THE WILD WHITE WHALE was published by Small World Publishing.

The history of Raoul Wallenberg moved me and for years I collected articles. His bravery and heroism compelled me to write this story.

GREAT SAVE!

*I*t is wartime in Hungary. A tall man watches as those in the Death March file past. He pulls out some prisoners wearing a gold star sewn on their coats. The Nazi commander rushes over, pointing his gun. "What is the meaning of this?"

The man hands the commander Swedish passports. "Swedes. These people are mine," he says, matter-of-factly.

They are saved!

One of the saved prisoners kisses his hand. "You're an angel."

The angel is Raoul Wallenberg.

Nathan passes me the puck. I have an opening. I shoot and...miss. "Wake up, Raoul," Nathan, our captain, yells at me.

No time to sulk as the puck is passed up the line and the Smashers score. We're down by one. The clock is ticking. Here's my chance. I'm hit with a clean pass, fake a pass to Sid, then take a slap shot. Ooh! Just wide!

Nathan gets the puck. I'm open, but he won't pass it to me and give me another chance. My best friend has turned on me. He's small, but fast and goes in for the kill. We score! We're tied at one all.

The rest of the game, no one will pass to me. I

CHAMPION

get the puck and decide to go for it, but Sid—my own teammate—steals the puck from me. I can't believe it! Things sure are screwed up in this game. Sid snaps the puck in the five hole, right through the goalie's legs. We're ahead two to one. Way to go Lightning.

The Smashers get control of the puck and we can't get near it. It's the third period with seconds to play. Tommy, from the visitor's team, gets a break away and backhands it top shelf. I hold my breath. The puck is snapped out of the air by Mark's goalie's glove. The Lightning jump all over Mark. We win! My adrenaline pumps. Life is great.

"We'll beat ya' next game," yells Tommy from The Smashers. "There is no next game," says a small voice. We all turn and stare at scrawny, shy Sheldon.

"What are you talking about, man?" asks Nathan.

"The government sold this land," says Sheldon.

"No way," I cry.

Sheldon shrugs. "The rink is history. It's going to become a parking lot for some restaurant chain."

"Who told you?" I ask.

"My father, that's who. He found out that your father's law firm sold it for the city."

"I don't believe it," I say.

"You better believe it, Raoul," says Sheldon. "Ask your father."

"How dare you blame my father!" I swing at Sheldon's face, but Sheldon ducks and Nathan holds

me back. Besides, it would be a slaughter. I could cream Sheldon with one arm tied behind my back.

"They can't do that," says Sid.

"Yeah," the Lightning echo.

"It's already done," says Sheldon.

My fingers shake as I take off my skates. I go straight home. The others leave too. No one is in the mood for a victory party. I'll prove to Sheldon that my father could never do that in a million years.

I charge into the living room. "Where's Dad?" I ask, more like a command really.

Mom points a finger at me. "Take off your boots. You're dripping snow everywhere."

I take them off and come back in. "Where is he?" I demand.

"He had to go out of town on business," says Mom.

I raise my voice. "I need to talk to him."

"Shh." She points to Grandma who is lighting a candle. She waves her hands across the flame, muttering a prayer. Now she is crying.

"Did someone die, Mom?"

"Raoul Wallenberg," she whispers. "Grandma's lighting a Yahrzeit Memorial Candle to remember him by."

"Why?"

"Later." She points at Grandma who is rocking

·CHAMPION·

back and forth as she cries. Mom takes my baby sister from the cradle and rocks her. Always "later". I storm out and go to my room. Once a year, Grandma goes through the ritual with the candle and cries nonstop, while Grandpa prays a lot and Mom acts all mysterious. I'm tired of not knowing. If nobody will tell me, I'll find out for myself.

After a while, I head back to the dining room. Grandma serves Grandpa first. It's my favorite, paprikash chicken. I take the leg. Mom holds the baby, trying to eat with one hand. The silence at dinner is suffocating.

"Why won't you talk to me about Raoul Wallenberg?" I complain, the words coming out louder than I wanted.

Mom's eyes go wide. Grandpa slams his fist on the table. "No raise voice!"

"Sorry, Grandpa," I apologize. "But why is it such a secret? Please tell me about the man I'm named after?"

"Later." He looks up as the tears well around my grandmother's eyes.

I lose my appetite. "Fine. Then I think I'll wait for *later* in my room." I shove my full plate aside and run to my room. I fling myself onto my bed, landing on something hard. I pick it up and examine it. It's my history book.

My stomach rumbles. I have to talk to Dad.

I can't bring myself to go out there again and apologize.

I open the book and begin to read about World War II, hoping that if I really get into it, my hunger pangs will be forgotten. Hitler and the Nazis believed that the Aryan race—the Germans— were the future of mankind. Anyone not blonde and with baby blues was an enemy of the State. Anyone the Nazis felt was not perfect, had to be destroyed. Jews and gypsies had black hair and brown eyes so they had to be exterminated. Homosexuals and the retarded were not "perfect" so they had to be killed too. Lots of people suffered. But only the Jews lost six million people. Most were killed in concentration camps, some shot, others sent to gas chambers, or beaten to death. Many died of starvation and disease.

I'm beginning to think that my problems are downright babyish compared to what went on during the War. I know this is a history book—a schoolbook—but I can't put it down.

Around 11:00 my Mother goes to bed. I wait for her to fall asleep. I have a plan.

Carrying my flashlight, I climb the ladder to the attic. I lift the trap door. It creaks. Quickly, I switch off my flashlight and close the door. I can hear Grandpa shuffling along as he goes to the bathroom. I hold my breath. Thankfully, he doesn't hear too well. My flashlight scans the room. It's full of

trunks, old furniture and boxes. The dust makes me sneeze and I walk right into a giant cobweb. Something moves and I jump. I nervously laugh when I see that it's only my reflection in a full length mirror. Sighing, I open box after box full of old clothes smelling of moth balls.

Nothing here. I don't know why I thought I would find something, some clue to my namesake. I sit down on a pile of books and look around. There must be 50 books written in Hungarian all around me. I start to read the titles. I've learned a lot of Hungarian from my grandfather. He spends weekends teaching me to read Hungarian. I lift one of the books and there it is. I know it's what I've been looking for. The family album. Tons of pictures, all with Hungarian news clippings taped beside them. The name Raoul Wallenberg stands out.

At last, the truth. One page sticks out. It has big black headlines.

WALLENBERG'S FATE STILL A MYSTERY AFTER FIFTY YEARS.

Where's Raoul Wallenberg, the greatest heroe of World War II? Is he dead? If he is, when And how did he die?

A hero? I'm named after a hero. My heart beats fast as I read on.

CHAMPION

Was he executed? Did he die in a Soviet prison? Did he end up in Siberia? Could he still be alive today at age eighty-three, having survived a horrible prison system this long?

I scratch my head. If he's a hero, why was he thrown in prison? Two stapled, browned and torn papers, flutter to the floor. Swedish passports. What does this mean?

A light shines in my eyes. Shocked, I drop the passports and stare into Grandpa's angry face.

"Vat you do dis hour?" He grabs the papers from me. "Ahh." His face softens as he examines the passports. "You vant to know da trut?"

I nod.

"I marched in a dead march vit Grandma, and two sons and tree daughters. Your Mom, vasn't born yet. Raoul didn't have much time and he just grab your Grandma and me. Vallenberg shoved dese false passports into our hands. "Svedes" he yelled as he pushed us past da guards. Raoul tried to save my children, but the Gestapo arrived and tings vere getting too dangerous for da ones already saved so Raoul took dose dat he had to safety. He saved our lives. Vitout him, your Mom never be born to have you and your sister. Da rest of my children, not so lucky."

157

CHAMPION

It's the first time I've seen Grandpa cry.

"Why such a big secret, Grandpa?" I say in a whisper.

"Grandma cries and carries on whenever I try to tell da whole story. Remembering her dead family is too painful. But your fader insists dat your name be same as man who saved our lives. Raoul Vallenberg. Of course you have to know. It is goot dat Grandma can't hear us right now. Vallenberg vasn't even Jewish and risked life. It is hurt to tink how he ended."

"I don't understand," I say.

"Nobody does. Da Russians tink maybe Raoul vas American spy and arrest him. Dey say he dead, but oder prisoners saw him. Ve hoped for so long. But too much time pass, and den dey find bones. Now we know he dead."

I climb into bed dreaming about an angel looking over me.

Waking up early the next morning, I rush to hockey practice. Sheldon and Nathan are fooling around on the rink. I go to put on my skates.

"Get lost. It's because of your father we're losing the rink," says Sheldon. Shy, quiet Sheldon all of a sudden has a lot to say. I wish he'd go back to the way he was. I liked him a lot better then.

Leaving quickly, so that they don't see the tears, I go to Sid's house. I'm surprised to see him still in pajamas. "Why aren't you at the rink?" I ask.

"What's the point in practicing if the rink is

being torn down?" asks Sid. "And it's all your father's fault."

"Why would he do such a thing? This is my rink too."

"Remember you didn't score last game? Maybe you didn't try because you already knew that the rink was sold."

"What?" I'd like to punch him, but he's way bigger and stronger than me. I pace around the room. "Sure I blew it last game, but I'm no quitter and I'd never sell out on the team." There's nothing more to say, so I go home. I'm bursting inside to talk to Dad, to hear him reassure me that he couldn't have sold the rink. He could never do anything like that. Could he?

I go to the kitchen where Mom is feeding the baby. "Eat." She brings me a stack of pancakes. Famished, I shove them in as fast as I can. "Raoul, we need to talk." I gulp. This sounds serious. My mother wrings her hands. "I was wrong not to tell you about Raoul Wallenberg."

"Mom, I understand. I'm proud to be named Raoul."

"That's why Grandma lights a candle each year. To remember Raoul Wallenberg. She also mourns my older brothers and sisters who couldn't be saved." A single tear slides down her cheek.

Grandpa walks in. "Dere's someting ve must do.

Come." The pancakes sit heavy in my stomach as I ride beside Grandpa in his beat up truck. We stop at a park. Grandpa leads me to a statue. "Dat's him, Raoul Vallenberg." I read the plaque. "Angel," says Grandpa, blowing his nose. We drive home in silence.

Mom looks at my sad face. "What's wrong, Raoul?"

"I realize now that if it wasn't for Raoul Wallenberg, I wouldn't be here today. He saved my life. All our lives. And we'll never have a chance to thank him," I say, sadly. I sit there in silence.

"Why don't you go play hockey. That always makes you feel better," says Mom.

"I can't."

"Why not?" asks Mom.

"Because the rink's been sold."

"Isn't there anything your team can do? Is there somewhere else you can play?"

"It's complicated, Mom."

"Complicated?" Mom echoes. "It's only complicated if you don't do anything. You know, your namesake, Raoul Wallenberg taught me an important lesson. He was only one man and he made a difference. Alone, he fought for and freed many Jews. I think that if you try, you can make a difference here."

"That's highly unlikely, under the circumstances."

"What could be so difficult that would make you not want to try?"

"Well, the team says that Dad's firm sold the rink and now it's being turned into a parking lot."

"What!" Mom cries. "And you believe them? You know full well your father would never do such a thing. And he certainly would have told us first, if, for some reason, he had to sell the rink."

"I don't know," I answer, remembering the time Dad told us we were moving, a day before camp started. "Couldn't resist buying the property. And we got a great deal on the house," he had told me.

"You know what," Mom says, clearly worried, "I'll call him right now. He's in a hotel at a convention in Detroit. We'll get to the bottom of this."

I nod. I get the feeling that Mom wants to prepare Dad before I start in on him.

"Raoul, pick up the phone," she calls. I take a deep breath. "Hello, Dad. Did Mom tell you?"

"Son, I didn't realize that it was your rink. It was just a property for sale," Dad explains. "It's what I do. I sell properties. I'm so sorry."

But I'm not buying it. "Sorry, won't bring it back. And sorry won't make the guys on the team hate me less. I gotta go."

I hang up. I'm trying hard not to cry. Mom looks like she's going to cry, too.

"I feel terrible, dear," she says. "But I'm sure

your father didn't realize it was the team's rink. You know how these things work. Someone contacts him and asks him to sell their property and he looks for buyers. Half the time he doesn't even see the property he's going to sell. I'm sure that—"

"I hate him," I cry, feeling my face get red.

"You're angry with him. I understand. I would be too. But if the land is already sold, I don't know if even Raoul Wallenberg could help you."

"I pick up the phone and dial Sheldon. "Who bought the land?" I ask him.

"A Hungarian restaurant chain called Goulash."

Hungarian! "Thanks." I hang up, look in the phone book for "Goulash", and grab my coat.

"Where are you going, dear?" Mom asks, as she sees me head outside.

"I think I know what Raoul Wallenberg would do," I mumble as I rush out.

The cold, strong wind chills right through me, but I zip up my collar and walk against the wind six blocks to a tall building. In the lobby sits a security guard. I look at the directory and see the name I'm looking for.

Tenth floor.

"Excuse me, young man. Do you have an appointment?" asks the secretary.

"I'm here to see my ah, uncle," I lie.

"Mr. Farkas is your uncle?" she says, wondering whether to believe me or not. "I know all of Mr. Farkas' family. I never saw you before."

162
CHAMPION

"Well, I just came in from…from… Hungary." Once you lie, it gets easier to back it up with another lie. "My mother, his sister, told me to come in and surprise him." Well, now I've given him an entirely new family.

The secretary believes me, and gets really excited when I mention my mother, Mr. Farkas' make-believe sister. She rushes into Farkas' office.

Out he pops, like he's being attacked by ghosts.

"My sister?" he bellows.

I nod.

"Come in! Come in!" he beckons. I rush in, looking at the secretary who looks at me as though I'm a ghost.

Once inside, he goes behind his desk, sits down, and looks at me. I'm still standing, and starting to feel smaller by the minute.

"Now, who are you really?" Mr. Farkas says. "My sister died in the War. I saw her go to the gas chambers. And as she was only 13 at the time, it is highly unlikely you are her son. Or even her grandson."

I'm beginning to think this is not a good idea.

"I had to see you," is all I can mumble.

"Well, you've seen me," he gets up. "Now, if there's nothing else—"

"*Várjál!*" (Wait), I say in Hungarian. He stops.

163

CHAMPION

"So you really are Hungarian." He seems calmer now.

"Yes, my grandfather taught me Hungarian. I really do need to see you. I'm sorry I lied, but your secretary wasn't going to let me in. Please, please," I beg, "let me talk to you for just five minutes. Then you can throw me out."

Mr. Farkas points to a chair. *"Servus,"* (Welcome) he says. "What can I do for you?"

"You bought our skating rink on Maple Leaf Street. My hockey team has nowhere else to play. My father sold it to you, but he didn't realize it was our hockey rink. I'm sure I can convince him to give up the sale if you decide not to buy it."

"I'm sorry young man, but I've already bought it. I need it for my expansion. I understand that it makes things tough for your team, but there's a great deal at stake here for my company. We've been looking for months for exactly this property. There's nothing I can do."

He gets up to escort me out. I think of Wallenberg and how he didn't give up. He had a plan and he stuck to it. If he could convince the Nazis to let my grandparents go, I should be able to convince a fellow Hungarian to help us out.

"Várjál," I tell him. "What if I had a way for us to continue to play at the rink, and, at the same time, bring you more customers than you'll know what to do with?"

"Then I would say you are a very young genius.

How can you fill my new restaurant and still keep your rink? Go ahead. I'm listening." He sits back down.

"Here's my plan." I speak in Hungarian just the way my Grandfather taught me. Mr. Farkas looks very skeptical as I outline my just made up plan. But, as I continue talking, he moves forward, actually paying attention. My heart beats fast. Will he buy it?

"Hey, Raoul, get these pads on and move into the net," says Nathan.

"But I'm a forward," I say.

"Mark's home with the flu so we need you to cover for him."

I mumble to myself as I tie up the pads. It's only a practice so no big deal. Everyone lines up and takes slap shots at me. Whack! Whack! Whack! I feel like hiding, like I'm under attack as one puck after another comes flying at my head. I pray that the mask will protect me. Clang! One puck gets through. My head spins, but I still have all my teeth.

Enough warm-up. Let's play a short practice game," says Nathan. He divides us into scarves and no scarves. I'm glad that I'm a scarf because it's so cold. Sid's on my team and he controls the puck. All the action is at the other end of the rink, with Sid passing to Sheldon, back to Sid, back to Sheldon.

Keep the puck down at their net, I pray. As long as everyone is there, I won't look like an idiot by letting in goals.

Hey, what's going on? Lots of passes. My team keeps on losing the puck then getting it only to lose it again. Everyone looks cold and tired. Too many clumsy plays and too many missed shots. Oh no. Nathan's sister, Stefanie, keeps intercepting our passes. Boy, she's fast. But when she passes to Nathan, Sid grabs it. Now Stefanie has it again. Oh, no. She's moving down the line. Towards me. She's passed center, carrying the puck towards me. I can see her eyes inside her mask. She looks mean, like she wants to ram the puck down my throat. I crouch down, ready. Hey, she's only a girl, I say to myself. Whack! The puck is on the ground and moving fast. I throw myself down on it, but it whizzes by me into the net.

"Game over," cries Nathan.

"Hey, Raoul, great save," calls Sheldon.

I look bewildered. "But I let the goal in."

"I'm talking about you saving the rink!" cries Sid. All of my teammates slap me on the back.

"Everyone go next door for a cup of hot chocolate," says Nathan. I start to take my skates off.

"Not you, Raoul," says Nathan.

"Why not?" I ask.

"What if Mark's still sick for the game this weekend? We might need you to sub. You could use a little work on your goalie skills," says Nathan.

166
·CHAMPION·

"But...."

Nathan doesn't give me a chance to complain. He wrists the puck and it sails past me into the net.

Wallenberg never gave up and I won't either. I pass it back. "Try again," I say as I crouch low waiting for the shot.

Our team shirts now read Goulash instead of Lightning. After each game, we walk next door to eat at The New Goulash Restaurant. Customers park in the rink's parking lot. The restaurant is packed from all the parents and kids coming to watch the game. That was our deal. We'll play and then eat. With over 30 games a year, that means we'll be eating goulash an awful lot. But we love it.

Every night I say my prayers and thank my lucky angel—Raoul Wallenberg.

EPILOGUE

Wallenberg, a young Swedish diplomat, saved 100,000 Jews in Hungary during World War II, passing out false Swedish passports to Jews under the noses of the soldiers. Within a year, Wallenberg saved more Jews from Hitler's Holocaust than all the governments of the world combined.

His plaque reads:

167

·CHAMPION·

RAOUL WALLENBERG
1912-19??

A man with a heart whose courage knew no bounds.

A Guardian Angel of Human Life.

May his example be honored for all time.

A Swedish diplomat stationed in Budapest, Hungary from July 1944-January 1945. In the midst of the most terrifying period of the Holocaust, he risked his life on a daily basis and saved from certain death tens of thousands of Jewish men, women, and children. In fighting the Nazis and Hitler's accomplices, he was arrested, tortured, and swallowed up forever by Stalin's henchmen.

168

CHAMPION

BASEBALL BLUES

BY TOVAH S. YAVIN

Tovah S. Yavin

When my two sons were young, they loved nothing more than baseball. They watched it on television, collected baseball cards, and followed their beloved Baltimore Orioles through good years and bad. But there was nothing quite as wonderful for them as playing baseball.

My sons are grown now—one attending law school in the United States and the other attending medical school in Israel. But they still love baseball. In fact, the one in Israel (I won't tell you if it's Adam or Dov) plays for the Israel Baseball Association's Tel Aviv A's. An old injury has kept him from pitching, but he's batting over .400!!

I hope you enjoy reading "Baseball Blues".

BASEBALL BLUES

For as long as Adam could remember, he had dreamed of wearing an All-Star uniform, of being chosen to play with the best of the best in the league. Now, he wished he could rip it off and throw it away.

He sat at the edge of the long bench, his back turned to the field, and papers balanced on his lap. They could force him to be here, but they couldn't force him to participate.

"Hey, Adam!" A slim-built boy in a red uniform shirt plopped down on the bench next to him. "I see you made the Blues. I'm gonna have to warn my teammates."

"Hi, Joe." Adam twisted around, facing the field, but not really looking at the carefully mown grass or straight chalk lines marking the base paths. "Warn them about what?"

"Are you kidding? Your arm. Your pitching. They have a right to know what they're up against, don't they?" Joe gave Adam's right arm a light punch. Then, he rubbed it, like he could take away any damage he might have done. "Don't want to hurt that arm— even if it is going to make it tough on us Reds."

"Punch all you want," Adam mumbled. "I'm not playing. I'm not even a real All-Star."

"What do you mean by that?" Joe asked, but

171

CHAMPION

his question disappeared into the shouts of his team-mates calling him from the other side of the field. Joe shrugged and trotted away without waiting for an answer.

Adam watched the Reds take off in a line, lop-ing around the far edge of the outfield. He watched his own team, the Blues, doing calisthenics by the sidelines. He watched Mr. Richards, the *real* coach, dump equipment out of a large, green duffel bag.

"Want to help me with these bases?" Mr. Richards called, without looking up.

Adam ran over, grabbed one of the thick, stuffed base pads and dragged it to the spot marked for first base. He took his time because he wanted to re-member how it felt to walk across an All-Star field. The base paths had been finely raked. Soft puffs of dirt flew up to dust Adam's shoes as he walked. The outfield grass was smooth and short. And the sky was a perfect blue. Adam sighed and turned back to his work.

He pounded each bag in place, making sure it was secure and flat against the ground. By the time he'd finished, the Blues were ready for batting prac-tice. Players crowded around the bench, helped themselves to bottles of water, traded batting hel-mets, and joked. Adam gathered up his homework papers and moved into the grandstands.

"Pick one of the Ten Commandments," his as-signment read. "Discuss the commandment and how it has been a challenge in your life."

Adam sighed. A typical end-of-year assignment at his Middle School, the Silver Spring Yeshiva for Boys.

He thought about picking *"Do not steal."* Adam didn't steal, except for an occasional extra base, but he did sometimes forget to ask before he borrowed things from his brother's room.

"Do not kill," was out of the question. Adam had never killed anyone, even though his brother sometimes seemed like a tempting target.

"Do not lie." That lying thing had been a bit of a challenge this year.

"Why are you sitting in the grandstands, Adam?"

He looked up and was surprised to see his rabbi coming down the steps.

"Hi, Rabbi Schwartz. What are you doing here?"

"I came to see you and Dov play. Your dad said...."

"Dov." Adam interrupted. "Just Dov."

"But...." Rabbi Schwartz pointed at Adam's uniform shirt. "I'm confused."

"Oh, this," Adam crossed his arms against his chest. "They made me a coach. See," he twisted around to show the rabbi that the back of his shirt had the word COACH written on it, instead of a number like the real All-Stars. "They made me a coach

173

CHAMPION

because they all felt sorry for me."

"But, isn't being a coach better than being a player? Doesn't that make you the boss?"

"Yeah. I guess," Adam mumbled, digging his toe into the seat in front of him.

Rabbi Schwartz was just trying to be nice. But he didn't understand. Being a coach wasn't better than being a player. Nothing was better than being a player.

Rabbi Schwartz rested his hand on Adam's shoulder. "It's a nice day for baseball, though, isn't it?"

Adam didn't trust his voice enough to try to answer, so he just watched as the rabbi wandered off to talk with other people

Adam spread his papers out next to him and wondered what to write. *Do not tell lies.* That sounded simple enough, but nothing was ever really simple. What was a lie, anyway? Was it a lie to say 'fine' when someone asks how you are even if you're not really fine? Or is it okay to just figure that they don't really want to know?

Adam stretched his right arm, flexed his elbow a few times, then reached across his body, wrapping his hand over his shoulder. He could feel the muscles stretching from his back, across his shoulders and down to his elbow, and it felt good. He let his arm fall straight down at his side, shook it a little, wriggled his fingers, then stretched again. There was no pain. No pain at all.

Do not tell lies. What if no one asked and you didn't tell? Is that a lie? Is it a lie if it's something that you know you're supposed to tell?

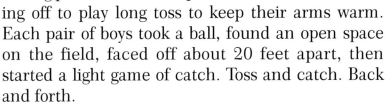

Adam really didn't want to think about that. Not today.

The Blues had finished batting practice and were pairing off to play long toss to keep their arms warm. Each pair of boys took a ball, found an open space on the field, faced off about 20 feet apart, then started a light game of catch. Toss and catch. Back and forth.

There were 15 players on the Blues, which meant that seven games of catch spread around the field. One boy was left without a partner and Mr. Richards waved for Adam to join him. Adam could think of nothing that he had ever wanted as much as being on an All-Star team. But not like this.

He made his way slowly down the bleachers and to the sidelines. Matt Campbell was the only player left and he was tossing his ball straight up and catching it, sending it a little higher each time. He nodded as Adam approached, then moved out to the center of the field without saying a word.

Adam and Matt quickly found a rhythm. A pause, a windup, a throw, a *whoosh* in the catcher's glove.

175

Adam was facing in the direction of his younger brother, Dov, who was working with the other Blues' catcher, Tim Jackson. Dov and Tim kept up a steady conversation that went back and forth to the same beat as the ball. Once in a while, they laughed. Adam watched them but was too far away to hear what they were saying.

"Thought you broke your arm." Matt finally interrupted Adam's thoughts.

"Elbow."

"You broke your elbow!"

"I didn't break it. I just had tendonitis."

"Tender what?"

"That means I overworked it. It needed rest. No cast or anything. I'm better now."

"Yeah? Are you playing, then?"

It was Adam's turn to send the ball back, and he put a little extra snap on it. Matt must not have been ready for that because the ball sailed past him before he even had his glove extended. Adam watched him retrieve the ball and move back into place.

Either Matt had forgotten his question, or he didn't care any more because Adam didn't answer and Matt didn't ask again. They threw the ball back and forth a few more times, then Coach Richards signaled for everyone to gather at the bench.

Coach Richards would want to review the game plan. He would talk about each player on the Reds, stressing his batting average and the kind of balls that he liked to swing at. If Adam had been pitching

176

CHAMPION

today, he would have listened very hard. But he probably wouldn't have heard anything that he didn't already know.

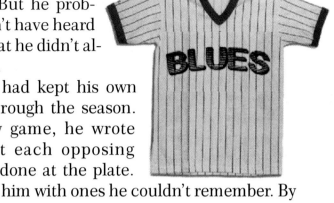

Adam had kept his own notes all through the season. After every game, he wrote down what each opposing player had done at the plate. Dov helped him with ones he couldn't remember. By the end of the season, the Silver brothers—Adam pitching and Dov catching—had come to be known as "the strike-out brothers." Coaches had even commented on how Adam always pitched such smart games.

Well, it wasn't just smart. That sounded like it was something that came to you without even trying. And nothing came to Adam without trying. He and Dov had been successful because they practiced and practiced and kept notes and reviewed their notes and planned and practiced and practiced.

But none of that mattered today. Today, Adam wasn't playing because he wasn't really an All-Star.

The stands were filling up. People ate peanuts and popcorn. They used their programs to point out particular players—probably their own sons. They smiled and laughed. It was a good day for baseball.

The umpire signaled for the teams to take the field. Dov moved into position behind home plate,

177

CHAMPION

and Adam shook his head. His little brother sure had turned out to be a good catcher. That was the one position that Adam had never even wanted to try.

Dov didn't seem to mind coming home bruised after every game. No matter how much gear the catcher wore, there were always balls that managed to catch a shin just below the leg guards, or clip a shoulder to the right or the left of the chest pad. And Dov never said a word.

And how did Adam's scrawny little brother manage to develop such a great arm? He was one of the few kids in his age range who could actually make the throw to second and occasionally, throw someone out trying to steal.

The Blues' starting pitcher was Jason Myers. He only had two fewer wins than Adam did during the season. He was accurate, but not fast. Dov would have to be very careful directing Jason's pitches.

The top of the first inning went well. Two batters went down on fly balls. One got a walk. But that didn't matter because the next Reds' batter struck out.

Now it was the Reds turn to take the field and the Blues were at the plate. Ben was batting first for the Blues. He was good—very good. Adam had always hated pitching to him during the regular season. Ben hit the only triple that Adam had given up all year.

Adam had worried a lot about that. Nervous-

·CHAMPION·

ness could really do a pitcher in and Adam feared he'd give up home run after home run if he ever got in an All-Star game. Of course, all that worrying turned out to be a waste of time. Adam could be as nervous as he wanted to be today. It wouldn't affect the way he did his job as a *pretend* coach.

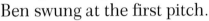

Ben swung at the first pitch.

"That's okay, Ben," Coach Richards called out. "Just settle in, wait for your pitch."

Ben swung at the second pitch, too, which was way too low.

"Look 'em over now, Ben," Coach Richards said. "Be selective."

He did look over the next one. Unfortunately, it was a perfect strike, right down the middle.

Adam could almost feel himself swinging away on that one. He could hear the tin ring of the metal bat on the ball. He could feel his own legs digging in, pushing off, trying to beat the ball to first base.

Ben just rolled his bat up against the cage surrounding the Blues' bench and slunk off the field.

"You'll get your hits," Adam said quietly. "You were just nervous."

"Yeah, I guess," Ben answered, shaking his head.

The Blues' second batter worked the pitcher

the way an All-Star player should. He watched the first pitch go by. Adam knew he would be trying to get a sense of the pitcher's motion and he'd be timing his throw. It was worth watching one pitch, even if it was a strike, to get that feeling that you understood the pitcher a little bit.

The batter also watched the second pitch go by, also, because it was an obvious ball. He made contact with the third pitch, just hard enough to send it skimming past the shortstop. The Blues' player was able to reach first base comfortably before the Reds had the ball under control and in the hands of the first baseman.

That gave the Blues their first runner. And Dov was up next.

Adam had to force himself to watch his little brother going up to hit in an All-Star game. But then, he couldn't take his eyes off him.

Dov had the athlete's walk. He was loose and lanky. One step flowed into the next. His arms swung gently at his side. He looked graceful, even when he was poised for the pitch, muscles flexed, eyes focused, and waiting.

Adam had never felt like that. He worried that his pitching motion was jerky. He felt awkward running out to the mound. And he wished he could swing the bat with the fluid motion of the players he saw on TV.

So, he worked on all those things. Pitching, running, hitting. He practiced and he read books and

he listened to his dad's advice. Lots more than Dov did.

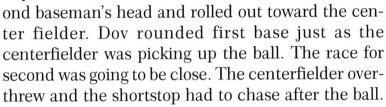

Dov swung at the first pitch. That boy would never learn.

Then, Adam realized that Dov had hit the ball and was running for first. The ball took a quick bounce over the second baseman's head and rolled out toward the center fielder. Dov rounded first base just as the centerfielder was picking up the ball. The race for second was going to be close. The centerfielder overthrew and the shortstop had to chase after the ball.

Dov's foot touched second base. The third base coach held both hands in the air signaling Dov to hold up. But Dov charged on, head down, arms pumping, legs stretched wide. The shortstop started to throw, but his feet slipped a little. He paused, set himself, and slung the ball toward the third baseman who was waiting with his foot on the bag and his glove outstretched.

"Slide!" Coach Richards screamed. And Dov slid, touching the base just as the ball thwacked into the third baseman's waiting glove.

No one cheered. No one clapped. The stands stood quiet as the referee threw his arms out to either side, hands flat, fingers spread.

"Safe!"

Dov lay sprawled across the dirt, his hand still on the base. He looked up at the referee.

"Safe," the ref repeated a little more quietly. He gave Dov a nod.

Now the crowd cheered. Adam could pick out his father's voice even with the whole Blues' team jumping, screaming, slapping each other all around him. The runner ahead of Dov had crossed home plate. The Blues had scored first. And Dov's batting helmet had flown off somewhere between first and second.

Coach Richards told the next batter to take his place at the plate and motioned for Adam to re-trieve the batting helmet.

Adam jogged out to the middle of the field, grabbed the helmet, and brought it to Dov.

"Hey, tell the coach I'm sorry," Dov whispered as he tugged at the helmet.

"Sorry? For...."

"You know, for swinging at the first pitch. I couldn't help myself."

Adam started back toward the bench.

"And I should have held up at second. Tell him I'm sorry about that, too," Dov added.

Adam stopped, swung around and stared at his little brother.

"Okay. You're sorry you swung when you should have watched, and you're sorry you ran when you should have stopped. And should I tell him you're really sorry you got a triple and batted in the first

182

run of the game. Should I tell him that, too?"

"Well, you know what I mean," Dov mumbled.

Adam just shook his head, ran back to the bench and sat down. He told the coach nothing.

The next Blues' batter struck out, so Dov never did get a chance to score. He came up to bat again in the third inning, but walked. Adam barely even got to see that because he'd been sent to the side of the field to warm up the next Blues' pitcher.

He and Jeff started by lobbing the ball back and forth to each other. They didn't talk much because even though they weren't throwing hard, this was serious business. Finally, Adam strapped on catcher's gear to let Jeff really work his arm.

Jeff had good speed, but he was wild. Adam had to scramble for the ball on every other throw.

"Sorry!" Jeff called out as Adam ran after one wild pitch.

"That's okay. Might as well get over your wildness, now. You'll settle down when you get in the game."

Adam scooped up the ball before it could roll under the stands. As he jogged back to his position, Jeff moved forward to meet him.

"Teach me how to throw a curve," Jeff said quietly when Adam held the ball out to him.

"What?"

"Show me how to throw a curve."

"I can't do that." Adam got down into his crouch, but Jeff hadn't moved.

"Why not. You know how, don't you?"

"Well, sort of. But...."

"Come on! Help me out."

Adam stretched to his feet again and sighed.

"First of all, you don't have time."

"Yes, we do. We can take ten or fifteen minutes, if we want. Just give me some pointers."

Adam laughed. "I spent hours and hours learning to throw a curve and barely had it working. And I shouldn't have...."

"I know. I know." Jeff nodded. "My dad told me you hurt your shoulder doing it."

"Elbow."

"But, you're better now, right."

"Look, Jeff. I'm better now because I quit trying to throw curves. We're not old enough. It strains your arm a lot more than just throwing straight and we're not ready for that. My dad says to wait until I'm 16 or 17."

"But if I just throw it today, I won't get hurt."

"You can't learn it today. Just throw straight and hard."

"See. That's the problem. I can either throw straight or I can throw hard. But I can't do both. If I

throw slower, these guys will hit every ball." Jeff looked out toward the field and shook his head.

"How's it going guys," Coach Richards called over.

Adam just waved, then motioned for Jeff to get back into position.

"Throw a strike," he told Jeff. "Even if you have to throw it slower."

Jeff did that, sending his pitch squarely into the middle of the strike zone. Then, Adam worked with him for a while, placing the ball a little higher or a little lower, moving it to the inside and then to the outside.

Adam was facing toward the field when he saw the Reds running in to their bench. He knew the third inning had ended. It was time for Jeff to pitch.

Adam started toward the Blues' bench, but Jeff hung back.

"I don't think I'm ready," he pleaded.

"You'll do fine."

"No. I won't. I'm going to get killed."

Adam put his arm on Jeff's shoulder and gently pushed him toward the bench. "You just need to place your pitches, carefully. Let me talk to the coach. But listen, that's how you have to practice. The way we were just doing it. You'll be lots better next year."

"Yeah," Jeff nodded. "If I only had somebody to

185

practice with. You're lucky to have a brother."

Jeff kept walking, but Adam had stopped.

Lucky he had a brother.

What did Jeff know? Sure, it was nice having a brother to practice baseball with. But what about last spring? What about that day that he begged Dov to catch for him while he worked on learning to throw a curve.

Dov knew Dad had said Adam was too young to learn the curve. Dov knew the coach had agreed. Sure, Dov said he didn't want to do it. But then he did it anyway. Why hadn't Dov just stuck to his word and refused.

Okay, so Adam had begged. Of course, he'd begged. And at the time, he'd hated Dov for making him beg.

That was such a great day. Even with all that happened later, it was still a great day.

Adam thought about how he'd felt the first time the ball actually did curve out and then back, right into Dov's glove. They had both just stared at each other, without saying a word.

Then, Dov leaped to his feet and shouted, "Did you see that? Did you see it?" Adam could almost hear him now. Dov had waved his hand through the air to show just how the ball had gone. Straight. Then out. Then back again. Right into the glove.

That was such a great day. And then they practiced and practiced and practiced. They kept at it for a couple of hours. Adam only managed to make

about a dozen pitches actually work. But that's what it took. Practice. Practice. Practice.

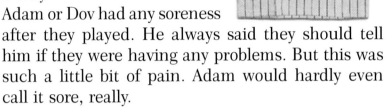

It wasn't until that night that Adam's elbow had started to ache. Just a little, at first, so he ignored it. Dad always wanted to know if Adam or Dov had any soreness after they played. He always said they should tell him if they were having any problems. But this was such a little bit of pain. Adam would hardly even call it sore, really.

He woke up in the middle of the night with his elbow throbbing, and his fingers tingling as if needles were dancing across his hand. He realized, then, that they'd made a mistake. He should have listened to Dad—and the coach. Adam decided, lying in bed that night, trying to rub the pain away, that he'd learned his lesson. He would save the curve ball for when he got older. For now, it would just be fastballs and change-ups.

By morning, he could hardly move his arm. Adam thought he could hide it. He thought that if he could just get through that day, he'd be fine again. But Dov told.

Dov told Dad, Dad told the coach, and Adam wound up at the doctor's office. The doctor said he'd be fine if he let his arm rest for a while.

Everyone acted so relieved when they heard that; Dad, Mom, Coach, and Dov. But Adam understood what that meant. It meant baseball season was over for him. Right along with his chance for All-Stars.

Dov was fielding Jeff's warm-up pitches when Adam took his place on the bench. His notebook had fallen to the ground. He picked it up and wiped away a splotch of dirt.

"How did Jeff look to you?" Coach Richards asked.

"He's slow, coach. He can't control the ball when he throws hard."

"I know. I know. But Jason can't pitch more than three innings. And we're up two runs. Maybe, he can hang on for us."

Coach looked hopeful, but Adam had a bad feeling.

Joe was the next Reds' player to bat. Adam watched Joe moving to the plate and could see in his mind, just as clearly as if he was holding it in his hands, a page from the notebook that he and Dov had kept all through the season.

Joe Taylor. Strong hitter. Very impatient.

"Coach," Adam said. Coach Richards was staring intently at the field and gave no sign that he'd heard Adam.

"Coach!" Adam raised his voice.

"Mmm. What, Adam?" the coach answered without looking.

"Jeff should try to throw balls. No strikes."

188
CHAMPION

"No strikes? Why?"

"Because Joe is a real impatient hitter. He swings by the third pitch, no matter what you throw him."

The coach was silent, staring at Adam.

Adam nodded. Jeff was set to pitch. Dov was set to catch. And Joe was set to hit.

"Time!" Coach Richards yelled.

The umpire gave him a nod and all the players relaxed as Coach Richards jogged out to the mound, motioning for Dov to follow. Adam watched as the coach rested his arm on Jeff's shoulder and leaned in close to talk.

Adam could almost feel it. The weight of a coach leaning against you, the weight of the ball in your hand, the weight of a game depending on you, eyes watching from the field, the plate, the stands, wondering what you were going to do next.

Adam loved it. Loved everything about it. Loved being in the middle of it. And hated watching it from the bench.

The conference ended. The coach and Dov returned to their places. Jeff made his pitch. Too high. Joe watched that one. But he couldn't hold himself back from the next three, even though Jeff kept the pitches well out of the strike zone. Joe struck out.

189
CHAMPION

After that, Coach Richards asked Adam about each batter as they came to the plate. Jeff couldn't keep them all from hitting, but he did get through the inning and only gave up one run. He gave up another one in the top of the fifth making the score tied.

The Reds were sending out a new pitcher for the bottom half of the fifth inning, which gave Coach Richards a little time to talk to his team.

"Jeff's doing a good job out there," he began. "The Reds are tough hitters and he's kept the lid on things for us. Now, it's time for *us* to be tough hitters. We've got to make something happen during this inning."

Adam felt a drop of rain hit his hand. He wiped it away and focused on the coach.

"We need to put a couple of runs on the board—this inning—so that Jeff can put the game away in the sixth."

Another drop landed on Adam, this time on his face. And a few more on his arm. Then came the steady patter.

Coach Richards looked across the field to the umpire. Within a couple of minutes, the rain was falling steadily and the umpire had motioned for all the players to move off the field. Everyone hustled to the sheltered area under the stands.

Four and a half innings could be a complete game in this league, since the games were a total of six innings. But not in an All-Star game with a tied

score. Everyone settled in for the wait.

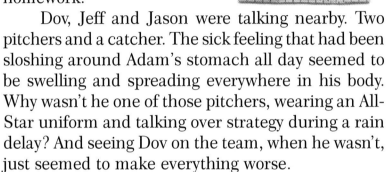

Groups of players huddled together while the spectators talked and bought snacks. Adam found a place to sit in a quiet corner and decided it was time to make a little headway on his homework.

Dov, Jeff and Jason were talking nearby. Two pitchers and a catcher. The sick feeling that had been sloshing around Adam's stomach all day seemed to be swelling and spreading everywhere in his body. Why wasn't he one of those pitchers, wearing an All-Star uniform and talking over strategy during a rain delay? And seeing Dov on the team, when he wasn't, just seemed to make everything worse.

Adam opened his notebook. *Don't lie.* He had sort of lied when he decided not to tell anyone about his sore elbow. He would never admit this out loud, but he'd been a little glad when Dov told and Mom took him to the doctor. And, he'd been very relieved to hear that his arm wasn't going to be injured forever.

So, he could choose "lying" for his topic. But somehow, it didn't feel right.

Adam realized that he was struggling with something right now. But lying wasn't the only thing gnawing at the pit of his stomach. What was it? What

191

was he feeling? Anger? Disappointment? Jealousy?

"Hey, Adam," Jeff said, leaning against the wall next to Adam. "Dov was telling me all about how you learned to be such a good pitcher."

"I'm not so good."

"He said you just about killed your garage door practicing. I mean, until you got your control. That's what he said."

"Yeah. We practiced a lot. Used the garage door as the back stop." Adam laughed. "Dad wasn't too happy." He looked up and realized that Jeff wasn't really listening to him. He was staring off at the crowd around the snack shops.

"Think I should get a hot dog?" Jeff interrupted.

"Naah. I wouldn't," Adam looked out at the rain that was falling slower now. "This is going to stop and you'll probably finish the game. I wouldn't eat."

"Smells so good though."

Adam just shook his head as Jeff wandered off towards the hot dog stand. He flipped open his notebook and scanned down the list of commandments again. He just didn't feel like writing about lying. What else was there? *Honor your parents. Don't covet.*

Dad and Rabbi Schwartz came by. They talked to Adam about the game for a while, then left. Joe and a few other Reds' players came by after that. By the time they left, the rain had stopped and Coach Richards was calling the Blues together.

Adam joined the team just in time to see the

coach leading Jeff to a nearby
table. Jeff was doubled
over and groaning.

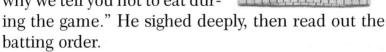

"Sit here. Drink a
soda. Maybe, you'll feel better by the time we start the
sixth." Coach Richards shook
his head and looked toward
the sky. "You see, boys. This is
why we tell you not to eat dur-
ing the game." He sighed deeply, then read out the
batting order.

Everyone, except Jeff, filed back onto the field
and to the Blues' bench. Several fathers were still
helping the umpires spread kitty litter around home
plate and over puddles along the base paths.

Adam breathed deeply. The air smelled of grass
and mud and popcorn. There was a slight, cool breeze
and the sky now had streaks of pink and white
blotches criss-crossing its clear blue. A perfect baseball afternoon.

Except that Dov was getting ready to bat and
Adam was getting ready to sit. *Don't covet.* What
had the rabbi told them last week about coveting?
He said it didn't mean just not to want things that
somebody else had. It meant not wanting to be what
somebody else was—smarter, stronger, better looking. The rabbi said that God gave everybody special
talents and abilities. When you wished you were like
somebody else, you were being ungrateful. It was

like getting a gift and then wishing that it had been something different.

The rabbi said to be satisfied with the way God made you and do the best you could with it. He said not to covet the gifts that God gave to somebody else.

You weren't supposed to wish you were wearing the uniform that somebody else was wearing on a perfectly perfect baseball afternoon in an All-Star game.

Don't covet. Adam definitely needed to work on that commandment. And there was plenty he could write about it, too.

The umpire signaled for the game to resume. Dov stepped to the plate. He swished his foot across the newly spread kitty litter, hitched his shoulders, stretched his neck, then stepped in and waited for the pitch.

The Reds' pitcher launched a solid strike and Dov swung. That boy would never learn. How many times had the coach said not to swing at the first pitch?

But Dov swung and sent the ball skittering out to the center fielder. A stand-up double. Adam just shook his head.

The next Blues' batter struck-out. Jason was up next. He hit a long fly to right field. The ball was caught, putting Jason out, but Dov made it easily to third.

Matt came up next. He was the weakest hitter

194
·CHAMPION·

on the Blues. If Jeff hadn't still been behind the stands groaning and holding his stomach, Matt wouldn't even be in the game.

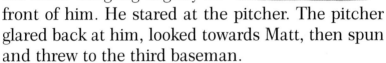

Matt entered the batter's box, and Dov took a few steps off third base. Dov leaned forward, legs spread wide apart, his arms dangling slightly in front of him. He stared at the pitcher. The pitcher glared back at him, looked towards Matt, then spun and threw to the third baseman.

Dov scrambled back to the base.

Matt took two practice swings and crouched, waiting for the pitch. The pitcher wound up. Dov moved off third base. He took a step off the bag as casually as if he'd been going for a stroll. Then, he hunched over and took two more broad steps, hopping sideways.

The pitcher looked at Dov. Dov stared back and took another side-ways hop toward home plate. The pitcher looked toward Matt, back at Dov, then spun and threw to the third baseman.

Dov dove, stretching his body back towards third, reaching out and brushing it with the tip of his finger just as the ball smacked into the third baseman's glove.

"Safe," called the umpire.

But just barely, thought Adam. You'd better be

195
·CHAMPION·

careful, Dov. Better be careful.

Dov held still for a moment, sprawled across the dirt, his finger still touching the bag. He looked up at the umpire, and the umpire called time.

Only then did Dov stand up. He brushed off his uniform sending out sprinkles of kitty litter, then planted his foot on third base.

Matt stepped in again, ready to bat. The pitcher looked at his catcher again, ready to pitch. And Dov took a step off the bag.

Two quick hops and he stopped, hunched over, watching the pitcher. The pitcher watched him. Dov took another hop, leaning slightly toward home plate.

The pitcher spun and threw, sending the ball high over the head of his third baseman. It smacked into the wall of the stands, bounced back and rolled into the third baseman's waiting glove.

Too late.

Dov had already crossed home. The Blues roared off the bench. They ganged up around Dov, slapping his back and pounding on his batting helmet.

Adam stayed on the bench.

The coach called for the team to settle down and Matt stepped in to finish his at-bat. Mr. Richards waved for Adam to join him and Dov. Adam didn't want to, but he went anyway.

"We might not have much time," Coach Richards began. "Jeff is still sick. I'm going to let Dov pitch the last inning. Adam, I need you to warm him up."

"But, Dov isn't...." Adam's voice trailed off. Dov wasn't a pitcher. He was just a catcher. And, apparently, a pretty good runner. But a pitcher? This wasn't fair. It just wasn't fair.

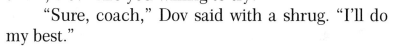

"I know he hasn't pitched much. But we don't have much choice. What do you think, Dov? Are you willing to try?"

"Sure, coach," Dov said with a shrug. "I'll do my best."

Dov grabbed a ball and the two brothers moved off to the side of the field. They started just as Adam and Jeff had started—throwing easy, getting a feel for the distance, without trying for speed. But Matt already had one strike, so they quickly got serious.

Dov had some snap in his throw, although nothing like the speed or accuracy that Adam had worked so much on during the season. Still, he wasn't so bad.

"I wish I didn't have to do this, Adam."

"Do what? Pitch the final inning of the All-Star game. Probably win and be the big hero. I can see why you wouldn't want to do that."

"But what if I don't win? What if I make us lose?"

"Well, first of all, the Blues are up one run— thanks to you. And even if you do lose the game,

you're not really a pitcher. No one will blame you. They'll more likely blame Jeff for stuffing himself on hot dogs in the middle of the game and getting himself sick."

Dov laughed as he made his last pitch. "Yeah, I guess. Anyway, looks like Matt struck out."

Adam turned toward the field in time to see the Reds running off. He looked back at his little brother, who was looking just a little sick, himself.

"Hey, you're going to be fine."

"I don't know," Dov stared down at his feet. "I'm really not a pitcher. I wish it was you going in."

"Yeah, me too. You don't know how much I wish that. But it's not me. It's you. So, just go in and do the best you can."

Adam clapped Dov on the back and Dov took off, loping toward the pitcher's mound.

The lead batter swung at Dov's first pitch, connected, and sent it flying far out towards centerfield. The Blues' fielder backed up threes steps and extended his glove.

Adam leaped to his feet, forgetting that he really didn't care how this game ended, and that it wouldn't be such a bad thing if Dov lost this game for the Blues. He'd had a pretty good run already today, for a kid brother. He strained to see the ball as it plunked down, just as pretty as could be, right into the center fielder's glove.

"Yes!" Adam pumped his fist, then remembered that it was Dov out there and not him. So he sat

198
·CHAMPION·

back down on the bench.

The second Reds' batter struck out even though Dov was lobbing in soft, fat strikes.

Bottom of the Sixth. Two outs. One more and Dov would have this game won. Adam just couldn't believe Dov's luck, until he noticed who was coming up to bat next.

Roy Roberts.

Just about the best hitter in the league. Maybe, just maybe, Dov's luck was about to run out.

Adam leaned back, wrapped his hands behind his head, and stretched his feet out far in front of him. He knew just how he would pitch to Roy, if he were the one on the mound. But it was Dov out there, and Adam felt sure that Dov didn't have a clue how to get this guy out.

Adam was right. Dov brought the first pitch as hard as he could right down the middle. But it wasn't hard enough and Roy launched it towards left field, barely crossing the foul line.

"Strike one!" the umpire screamed.

Okay, Dov, Adam thought. You got out of that one—but you've got two more to go. Let's just see what happens.

Dov's next pitch was so high, it almost sailed over Roy's head. Roy watched it go by for ball one.

Dov dropped the next pitch, a little, but not enough to be a strike. Roy watched that one go by, too.

Dov dug his toe into the pitcher's mound. He twisted his foot from side to side creating a shallow hole, then slipped his foot into the hole and tensed his body to make the next pitch.

So that was it, Adam almost said out loud. You haven't struck out this guy because the mound was a little too smooth. That little hole ought to do it. Go for it, little brother.

Dov looked over at Adam, almost as if he had been reading Adam's mind. Adam gave him a nod and Dov looked at his catcher. A moment later, Dov relaxed his arms and stepped back again.

He looked toward Adam, swept his foot across the hole that he'd dug in the mound and moved into position again.

Adam was almost enjoying watching Dov squirm. He leaned back and knocked his notebook with his homework assignment to the ground. When he bent to pick it up, he saw written in his own messy script—*Don't Covet things or people.*

Don't covet other people. Don't wish you were like someone else because God made everyone special in their own way. That's what Adam was planning to write. His rabbi would love it.

Adam sighed. He knew what he was going to write for his assignment, all right, but he also knew just what he had to do.

"Time!" Adam screamed just as Dov was ready

for his wind-up.

"Time?" the umpire repeated. "Did someone yell time?"

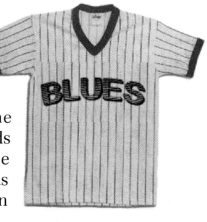

"I did." Adam jumped up and strode towards the mound before Coach Richards could say anything. For the first time that day, Adam was glad to have COACH written across the back of his shirt.

"What should I do?" Dov asked as Adam came near.

"Pitch him low."

"Low?"

"That's the only bad stuff he'll swing at and he'll kill you if you throw him strikes."

Dov slapped the ball into his glove. Once. Twice. "Are you sure?"

"Of course, I'm sure." Adam reached for his back pocket because that's where he'd carried his notes on every hitter in the league during the season. There were no notes there today, so Adam just patted Dov's back. "I'm sure. Keep 'em low."

Dov's next pitch was so low it almost bounced in the dirt. Roy swung anyway and his entire bench groaned. Dov made the next pitch look a little better, but it was still low and well out of the strike zone. Roy swung and missed.

The Blues exploded off their bench when the

umpire called strike three. All except Adam. He stayed where he was and watched as his little brother was surrounded by his screaming teammates.

Adam looked up into the stands where he knew his father was sitting. Dad was cheering, too, and smiling, but he wasn't looking at Dov. Dad was looking at Adam.

Adam gave his father a wave, then ran out to join the other Blues at the mound. When Dov was hoisted into the air, it was Adam's shoulder that he sat on. And it was Adam's cheers that could be heard over all the others.

THE DOOTSCH

BY CRAIG LEWIS

Craig Lewis

The idea for this fictitious piece grew out of a true story I heard that occurred at the 2002 Maccabi Youth Games in Memphis, TN. Some members of the Memphis basketball team were nervous about an upcoming game, and one of the local rabbis passed by and convinced the boys to wrap tefillin before the game from which they ultimately emerged victorious. Whether or not there was a true connection is not for me to decide, but I found it to be an inspiring story of faith, ritual, and achievement.

As a first-year Rabbinical student at the Hebrew Union College, I have recently fufilled a dream of spending a year in Jerusalem and have even had the pleasure of coaching a youth baseball team in the Holy City.

THE DOOTSCH

Picture this. Two outs. Bases loaded. Bottom of the ninth in game seven of the World Series. At the plate stands none other than me, Robby Deutsch. On a 2-1 count I take a pitch for a strike just because I don't like 'em on the outside corner. I stare down the pitcher who has only blown one save in forty-five chances including six so far in the post season. The catcher gives the signal. The pitcher nods, goes into his stretch and delivers a 97-mile-per-hour fastball, belt high and inside. Just where I like it. CRACK! I crush it to right field, back, back, to the wall...and it falls into the right fielder's glove at the warning track.

The World Series just isn't won by guys named Robert Benjamin Deutsch. It's for guys like Derek Jeter or Luis Gonzales, at least since the old days when Sandy Koufax played. Unlike Koufax, Luis Gonzales even has a cool nickname to go with his World Series ring. They call him Lugo. The guys on my baseball team just call me the "Dootsch," but that's mostly because most of them can't figure out how to pronounce my last name. It's supposed to be "Doy-tch." It's German for German, or so I'm told. I don't really know. All I know is I would give just about anything to get a clutch base hit in a championship game. To be a hero.

205
·CHAMPION·

However, this season started out poorly for me and the Overly Auto Mall All-Stars. We lost our first five games, and I batted a lousy 0 for 12. It got so bad, Coach Conroy started letting me hit like once a game, and that was only at the end when he put me in the game because he had to. You see, our league has an "everybody plays" rule, so when the game was almost over, I got to see action. It wasn't like that before, though. I was never a knock-the-lights-out kind of hitter, but I have never, ever batted .000, not even in my worst nightmares. I'm a pretty good second baseman, and I usually get my share of hits, but the first part of the year, I just don't know. I hit a couple of line drives, but right at people. Once, the third baseman caught a ball I hit and immediately threw his glove off and started shaking out his hand. I thought he was gonna cry. I struck out a lot, too. I'd see the pitches I wanted, belt high and inside, and I just seemed to swing through them like there was a hole in my bat. In practice I stroked 'em good, but something mysterious happened at game times.

"Tough break, Dootsch," Coach Conroy told me after every game. "What did you eat today?"

He's not a doctor or a nutritionist. He just thought that whatever I'd been eating was bringing me bad luck. It wasn't like he was trying to get me on an athlete's diet of balanced protein, carbs and Power Bars. I could have eaten deep-fried tree bark covered in hot fudge and sardines, and if I went 3 for 4, he'd have told me to eat it again, every game

206
·CHAMPION·

day. I tried pizza, with thick and thin crust, tacos, milkshakes. I even tried an all-Cornflakes diet, but nothing worked. I just couldn't get into a rhythm. I also tried wearing a lucky pair of socks and T-shirt with my uniform but still got no results.

As if I wasn't already having a bad enough Spring with my baseball abilities going down the tubes, I also had to start Bar Mitzvah training. I had been very happy going to Hebrew school three times a week. Well maybe not "very happy." I was just fine with it, though. Then all of a sudden I had to start meeting with the Rabbi on Shabbat afternoons. I had to learn how to lead a service and how to chant the *Torah*. At first, it was the pits. And if I didn't have enough time for baseball practice, the games, and my homework, I had this extra chunk taken out of my weekend.

It wasn't like I didn't want a Bar Mitzvah. I really did. Yeah, there's the party and gifts and all that. Who wouldn't like that stuff? But it's a chance to stand up by yourself and to show people what you know. That you can do something important. To show that you're really good at something, something that you've practiced for, something you've earned. Rabbi Frankel says "It's kind of like going to the plate, but with a *kippah*, a *tallit*, and a *yad* instead of a helmet, a jersey, and a bat."

"To read from the Torah is one of the greatest

honors a young man can have," he told me on our first Saturday meeting. Of course he said that. He's a rabbi, but then he said something else that grabbed my attention. "If you want to do it well, it takes practice and repetition."

"Repetition." How many times did Coach Conroy tell us, "Boys go home and practice your swing. To be a good hitter, it takes practice and repetition." I told Rabbi how much he sounded like Coach. He said something very rabbinical like "Your coach speaks with much wisdom." It sounded like something from a movie and made him seem much older than he was. I swear that for just a moment I saw his clean-shaven face suddenly sprout a long, white beard. I wondered if he really meant it—that Coach was wise for using the same words to teach baseball as a Rabbi did to teach Torah. Or was he just being sarcastic?

He then said something that erased my doubt.

"The purpose of repetition in baseball is to swing again and again until it feels as natural as walking or breathing. You would never want to be in a batter's box facing, let's say, Randy Johnson and a 98-mile-an-hour split-seamer, feeling unsure of your swing. It would be awkward, and I guarantee he'd get you in three pitches. Now with Torah, and your Bar Mitzvah, you too want those words to be as natural as walking or breathing. Then, face to face with your family, friends, and congregation, you can look down at the scroll, open your mouth, and the words will

flow out smooth and effortlessly."

Then he asked me, "Are you familiar with George Brett?" I knew he was a
Hall of Famer, but I'd never seen him play.

"He was the only player to win batting
titles during three different decades," he told
me.

"The last was in 1990 I believe. No wonder you
never saw him play. Anyhow, there is a reason for
this babbling. His swing was so perfect, that even
when he missed, it looked like that was what he
meant to do. He would lean back on his left leg and
wait there completely motionless until the pitch
came. Then he would shift his weight toward the
front, guide his bat through the zone like water in a
gentle stream, and smack solid line drives into play.
He didn't even look like he was trying, but you would
be foolish to believe he wasn't."

"So if you're good at anything, you can make it
look easy?" I challenged.

"That's it. When everyone was watching, it
looked easy, those four or five times a game. But
hardly anybody ever saw the thousands upon thousands of practice swings that turned the art of hitting into a reflex action. Robby, that is what I hope
you will do with your Bar Mitzvah portion, so that
on 'game day,' you'll be ready."

It made sense to me. He made me accept that
it was going to take a lot of hard work to be Bar
Mitzvah-ed. I was going to have to practice every

week, like it or not, so that I would do well when the day finally came. Was I thrilled about it? Heck no. But then again, I wasn't always thrilled about hitting off a tee in my back yard or taking infield practice.

It was kind of funny. Funny that I never realized that Rabbi Frankel was a normal guy. I always figured he was too busy *"rabbi-ing"* to care about things like sports, but he really seemed like he knew his stuff. Also funny that Coach Conroy had been trying to teach me the secret of hitting, when all along, he was also teaching me the secret to reading the Torah. Since I couldn't just forget about my terrible slump, I had to wonder if becoming a Bar Mitzvah could help me get better at baseball. Our sixth game was coming the next day.

The thing about playing Sunday afternoon games is that there is never enough time to go home between Sunday school and the game, and you have to wear your uniform to class. That way you can leave straight for the ballpark and make it in time for warm-ups. Wearing your uniform around could be cool if you're a New York Yankee, but when you're on the winless Overly Auto Mall All-Stars, it's kind of embarrassing. So I tried to look as inconspicuous as possible when I walked into the classroom with my gray uniform with big, blue writing across the chest and a blue and white stripe on the pant legs. My cleats, with their laces tied together, hung off my shoulder. Under one arm I held my glove, and under the other was my hat. They won't let you wear

baseball hats in class—just *kippahs.*

Right behind me came Dave, our teacher. He was looking down at a book and not paying attention to where he was going When he bumped into me, knocking my glove to the ground, he said, "Oh excuse me. This must be the locker room. Can you tell me where my class is?" He thought he was funny. Teachers who want you to call them by their first name always think they're funny. I guess if we called Dave Mr. Morton, he wouldn't be able to crack his jokes. I wasn't in a laughing mood that day, but the rest of the class was.

They laughed a lot. I guess it was pretty funny, and Dave is actually kind of cool. I was just being grumpy because I felt stupid being there in my uniform and because I was nervous about the game. I picked up my glove and sat down at my desk.

Dave handed around the *tzedakah* box. I put in my quarter, and then it continued to be passed around. Dave took roll. He insisted that we answer in Hebrew, and if we didn't, he pretended like we weren't there. Since 'D' comes early in the alphabet, I got it over with and had time to gaze out the window and check the weather while he read the rest of the names. The sun was shining, and no clouds could be seen. Like the announcers on TV liked to say, it was "a beau-tee-full day for baseball." Once all fifteen names had been called, and everyone said *"poh,"* (here) Dave started the class.

"I want to talk about life after Bar or Bat-Mitzvah. What do you think happens, Shoshanah?" Dave pointed right at Shoshanah Lubow who just shrugged her shoulders.

"What about you, Robby?"

He caught me still looking out the window. I hate when teachers put me on the spot.

"I dunno," I answered. I was too busy thinking about the game to think about his question.

"'I dunno.'" He repeated my answer. "They never know," he told the ceiling like he was asking the heavens for help. "All I ever hear is 'I dunno.'"

Tyler Kaplan raised his hand. Tyler thought he was the smartest kid in the class. "Aren't we done?" he said when called on.

"No Tyler. That's just it. Kids like to think, 'Hey, I'm 13. I've done my Bar Mitzvah. I've got some cash...a bunch of checks for eighteen dollars. I'm done. Time to retire. Go to Miami and play shuffleboard and eat dinner at four o'clock and brag to all your friends about your family while in the same breath complain that they never come to visit.'"

Do you see what I mean about teachers who think they're funny?

"Is that what you want? Does it make sense?" he continued. I started to figure out what he was getting at.

My friend, Shalom Ofer, raised his hand.

"Yes Shalom. What do you think?"

"I dunno," he said innocently, and everyone

212

laughed, especially Dave.

When the room was quiet again, Dave explained his lesson. He told us that the day that we celebrated our Bar and Bat-Mitzvahs would be the end of the practicing, preparing, speech writing, and planning for that one day, but it was really the beginning of our "adult" responsibilities in the Jewish community. Adult my foot. We don't vote or drive or see the movies we want to. "PG-13" just isn't all it's cracked up to be. Dave could tell I wasn't buying it.

"You dare to doubt me, Robert Deutsch?"

I responded with a questioning stare.

"After your Bar Mitzvah, you can take part in one of the greatest *mitzvot* of them all. You can be counted in a *minyan*."

I knew what a minyan was. Ten Jews. The minimum required for public prayer. I didn't see what was the big deal.

"You see, what you don't realize is...."

Just then, Dave was interrupted by Rabbi Frankel.

"I hope I'm not too late," he said standing in the doorway. No one had even seen the rabbi come in. Dave told him he wasn't late, and asked him to join us.

"Thank you, David." He called him "Da-veed" with the Hebrew pronunciation like in the song about *"David Melech Yisrael chai chai v'kayom."* Just hearing it said like that made me want to do the hand motions to the song. I wondered why Rabbi Frankel was in our class since Sundays were usually spent only with Dave.

Rabbi Frankel took a blue cloth pouch from his pocket and unzipped the top. He held it out so we all could see what was inside.

"Does anyone know what these are?"

The pouch looked like a pint-sized tallit bag. I knew it wasn't that though. There was nobody pint-sized in our class, and the pouch's contents looked dark. The Rabbi pulled out a wooden box wrapped in a long strap that he unwound carefully. It looked kind of like what you might use to re-string a mitt. I knew it wasn't that either. On the other hand...Rabbi Frankel was a big baseball fan. No, there is no other hand, I told myself. Dave wouldn't give us a lesson on baseball mitts.

"These are *tefillin*," Rabbi Frankel explained and pulled another box from the bag. This one was bigger and had straps coming out from the sides and tied together in the back. After the knot the rest of the straps dangled freely. Rabbi Frankel put the box on his head and adjusted the knot so the box sat on his forehead right between his eyes. He then rolled up his left shirt sleeve and put the other box on his bicep. He tightened the loop that held it in place and began to wrap the strap around his arm making circles between his elbow and hand.

I knew what tefillin were. I had seen them in pictures. Tefillin were for older men, mostly rabbis.

They wore them when they prayed. The boxes had writings from the Torah on tiny handwritten pieces of parchment. Dave spoke while the Rabbi continued to wrap the tefillin around his hand.

"You all know how God commanded us to take these words and 'bind them for a sign' on our hands and how 'they shall be for frontlets' between our eyes."

"Just like in the *v'ahavta,* the first paragraph of the *Sh'ma,*" Tyler announced.

"Yes indeed," Dave confirmed and went on to explain how tefillin are to be worn during morning prayers, except on Shabbat and holidays.

"...and since you are all about to become Jewish young adults, we're going to teach you how to put them on."

Before I could even raise my hand to ask a question, Rabbi Frankel said, "I see that skeptical look on your face, Robby. They aren't just for old men or Rabbis. They are for everyone. In fact, Robby, why don't you come up here and be the first in your class to try these on?"

I tried to politely turn down the invitation, but I couldn't get out of it.

"Nonsense. You already have on short sleeves, so come on down!" Rabbi Frankel called, waving his hand. It was true—my baseball uniform was the only short-sleeved shirt in the class.

"You're the perfect victim—er I mean volunteer," Dave joked and everyone laughed again. I swear he must have been telling the same jokes his Sunday school teachers told, and their teachers before them, and before them, and before them.

I went to the front of the classroom and could feel everyone staring. A couple of my classmates, I don't know who, snickered. Rabbi Frankel carefully removed the tefillin from his arm and placed the box on my left bicep. It felt a little strange, and I was kind of embarrassed because I didn't know what I was supposed to do. When he tightened the strap, I started to ask if I was supposed to help, but he put his finger against his lips and shooshed me. He handed me a sheet of paper with two blessings on it, and while he wrapped the leather strap around my arm, I read the first. It wasn't easy to read, but I managed to sound it out. It ended with *"l'haniach tefillin"* (to put on tefillin.)

Rabbi then took the tefillin off his head and put it on mine. While he finished wrapping the arm tefillin around my hand, I read the second blessing. This one was a bit easier. After I finished saying *"al mitzvat tefillin"* (to do the commandment of tefillin) Rabbi Frankel patted me on the back, and said, "Now Robby, how does that feel?"

I only had one word to describe it: "Tight."

"It's supposed to be a little tight. You want it to leave a little reminder so that it will still be with you later in the day. It doesn't hurt does it, Robby?"

"Nah," I answered. "It just feels kind of weird."

216

CHAMPION

I helped Dave and Rabbi Frankel lead a short morning *tefillah*, and then it was time to go. A bell rang, and the other kids hurried out the door to join the chaos that always happened in the hallway at dismissal time.

Dave helped me take off the tefillin and put it back in the bag. Rabbi Frankel took his tiny bag, and told us both *"L'hitraoat* (goodbye)."

"Now was that so bad?" Dave asked me.

"Nah," I said. "I guess not." But I didn't have time for small talk. I had a game to play. I grabbed my hat, glove, and cleats and ran out the door.

"Good luck, Robby" I heard the words behind me. I didn't even have time to say, "Thanks. I need it."

My mom met me in the parking lot, and we sped off to the game. Waiting for me in the backseat was a tuna sandwich and a bottle of Gatorade. I devoured both in about five seconds flat. Eating so fast made it difficult to digest as we weaved in and out of the Sunday traffic, but I was in a hurry. When we got there, Mom dropped me off at the ballfield, and I saw my team already warming up. I joined them in the outfield.

"Hey Dootsch!" my friend Miguel shouted to me holding a ball above his head. He was the other second baseman on the team, but not quite as good a fielder, so he was usually used as a sub. I waved at him, and we started playing catch. Being around everyone in the same uniform as mine, with the whir

of the baseballs being flung back and forth, I felt I was where I belonged. I couldn't believe I endured an entire day of Sunday School in my Overly Auto Mall uniform. How embarrassing! The only thing that could embarrass me now was the way I played, and I had a feeling things might be changing for me real soon.

Coach Conroy came out of the dugout to talk to me. "Bad news," he said. "I'm going to start Miguel at second today. He's been hitting the ball real well."

"But coach, I'm feeling real good today."

"Don't worry, Dootsch, you'll get in the...." He stopped when he saw my arm. It had white circles on it from where the tefillin had been. "Dootsch, what's wrong with your arm?"

"It's nothing, Coach," I said not wanting to go into a long explanation about tiny scriptures in black boxes. I just wanted to focus on the game. "I'm ready to play."

I was going to get in the game. I had to. It was a league rule, but it probably meant I would get like one time at bat, and probably when it barely mattered. How was I supposed to break out of a slump that way? We were even playing the Rick's Reprographics Redbirds, and a blind one-armed dwarf could get a hit against those guys.

I just couldn't believe Miguel was going to start. What did Coach want? A bunch of booted infield ground balls just so we might get another hit or two? I couldn't help being a little mad at Miguel even

218
CHAMPION

though it wasn't really his fault. I took the ball and cocked my arm back, stepped forward and flung the ball as hard as I could. The ball flew directly towards Miguel's head. I shouldn't have done that. I knew he wasn't very quick with his glove. I was mad, but I didn't want to hurt him. Oh I was going to regret that. He put his glove up and the ball popped safely into the webbing in front of his face. Miguel had been practicing.

The dugout has to be the worst place to watch a game. Being so close to the field without really being in the game is so frustrating. I didn't like being one of the four players considered not good enough to start. Even worse I watched Miguel go two for two with a triple, a walk, and three RBIs. He even made a nice fielding play running to his right and picking up the ball behind the bag. An arching throw to Marty Biggins at first got the runner out by a foot. With Brian Shaw pitching the game of his life, not letting the Redbirds hit anything but ground balls and lazy pop-ups, the Overly Auto Mall All-Stars seemed unbeatable, and we had a 7-0 lead after the top of the fifth. It looked like Coach would have no reason to put me in the game until the very end when it probably wouldn't matter.

However, no one could have predicted what happened in the bottom of the fifth. The Redbirds' first batter battled Brian to a 3-2 count and then took a change-up that seemed to dance right over

CHAMPION

the outside corner. The umpire called it a ball. Even the batter was surprised, and I could see him grinning through the back of his helmet as he trotted to first base. The next batter stepped into the box, and the first pitch, a change-up, hit him in the ribs. There were runners on first and second.

"Looks like Brian's lost control of his change-up," I said to Coach.

Coach Conroy called time-out, and before he walked out to the mound, he told me, "Dootsch, that was a fastball."

Brian's arm was tired, and his pitches were losing speed and control. I wondered who Coach might choose as a relief pitcher. In our first five games, no one had really done a good job of it. Coach stood on the mound with Brian and our catcher Andy Ash. He put his hand on Brian's shoulder. I couldn't hear what the three of them were saying, but they all looked over to Miguel who slapped his fist into his glove. Coach patted Brian on the shoulder and came back to the dugout. Brian's next pitch bounced in the dirt and skipped past Andy. There were runners on second and third with no outs.

"I thinks it's time," Coach said to no one, and called time-out again. He walked to the mound, and Brian knew he was coming out of the game. He handed the ball to Coach who motioned for Miguel to come to the mound. Miguel was going to pitch? He'd never pitched before as far as I knew. I guess after losing five games in a row, Coach decided to

220

CHAMPION

try something new. That left a gap at second, and I knew I was the one who would fill it. Coach Conroy waved for me to come on to the field, and while Miguel threw his warm-up pitches, I fielded some practice ground balls. I was a little stiff from sitting, but I was more than ready to play.

With two runners on, Miguel pitched from the stretch, and fired the first pitch of his baseball career. It was a fastball, a good one, on the inside corner to a left-handed batter. The batter swung. A hot ground ball skimmed toward the gap between first and second. I moved to my left, scooped it up, and made a perfect throw to Marty Biggins for the out. The runner on third scored, but the guy on second had to hold. Not a bad start for old Miguel.

The next pitch, however...It wasn't really a bad pitch. The guy, who the other Redbirds called Moose, just got ahold of it and sent it to next year. It was 7-3, and before the inning ended, they dinked and dunked a few more hits to score two more runs. Things were getting uncomfortable.

Marty, our cleanup hitter, led off the sixth inning with a walk. Having taken Brian's number nine spot in the lineup, I knew I was guaranteed at least one chance to bat. There were just the questions of when and if the game would be on the line. Andy followed Marty's walk by hitting a ground ball to the second baseman who threw to the shortstop who then tossed the ball to first for an easy double play. Our

half of the sixth feebly ended with a lazy pop fly off the end of Marcus Millroy's bat. We had two innings left to protect our precious two run lead, but just one more chance to bat. That one chance was going to include a plate appearance by yours truly.

The Redbirds' first batter in the bottom of the sixth was Moose, and our whole team breathed a sigh of relief when he swung at and missed three straight pitches. Then Miguel turned around and pitched four straight balls. The batter after him slapped a single through the left side of the infield giving them first and third with one out. Then they cut our lead down to one run with a sacrifice fly to left field, and the runner moved from first to second when Joshua Jesse missed the cutoff man on his throw to the infield. Everything was falling apart.

Coach Conroy asked for a time-out and gathered the infielders around the pitcher's mound. "You know what to do boys," he said. "Just buckle down and remember what you've practiced." He went back to the dugout, and Miguel went into his stretch. The batter swung at the first pitch and hit a high blooper my way. I had to move back to catch it. I heard the center fielder's footsteps approaching, but I had a bead.

"Mine! Mine!" I called turning to attempt an over the shoulder grab. My feet pedaled and kicked up clouds of dust. The ball seemed to keep drifting. I saw it coming down and flopped on to my stomach with my glove extended as far as I could reach. The

ball hit the tip of my glove. "I caught it!" I thought, but saw the ball fall just in front of me. I popped myself up, grabbed the ball and heaved it toward home where the tying run slid into the plate. Miguel cut off the throw and chucked the ball to sec- ond where our shortstop Wes was covering the bag. The batter was trying to take an extra base. Wes swiped the tag down and made the third out.

The team breathed a collective sigh of relief. The game was far from over, but after blowing a seven run lead, we were feeling kind of low. The Redbirds put in a new pitcher for the top of the seventh, and this guy's warm-up pitches looked like smoke. You could barely see the ball from the time it left his hand until it popped into the catcher's mitt. We needed to score.

Our first batter, Joshua Jesse, struck out on three straight pitches. While I swung in the on-deck circle and tried my best to time the fastballs, I watched Andy Ash swing at and miss three straight pitches too. It came down to me. I stepped into the box, took a couple practice swings and readied my- self. The pitcher wound up, and before I knew it, the first pitch was past me for strike one. It didn't seem fair. I took another practice swing and waited for the next pitch. I started my swing early, but the ball went low and away. I looked kind of foolish swinging wildly at air. I called time, and stepped out of the box.

I rested the bat between my knees and wrung

CHAMPION

my hands together. I had to find a way to get a hit. I looked down at my arm and saw that the circles were still there. I must have really sensitive skin, or maybe Rabbi Frankel wrapped the tefillin a little too tight, after all. It made me think about what Rabbi had said, "practice and repetition." Then I thought about Coach Conroy saying the same thing. I closed my eyes and pictured myself swinging in the back-yard. It was the perfect swing. Over and over again, the bat sliced through the strike zone in my mind. The umpire called over to me and said, "Let's go, son." I nodded and stepped into the box.

I set my feet shoulder length apart and leaned back on my right leg. I didn't even have time to think. The pitch came. I swung, and the ball flew into the air. High to dead center. It cleared the fence by at least 20 feet. A home run! I sprinted around the bases and stomped on home. My teammates met me next to the plate. They were shouting, "Dootsch! Dootsch! Dootsch!" I was out of my slump. On my way into the dugout, Coach Conroy slapped me on the back and said, "Dootsch, whatever you did to-day, just keep doing it."

I had a feeling Coach might say that. I just rubbed my tefillin arm and smiled. After three more outs in the field, the Overly Auto Mall All-Stars cel-ebrated an 8-7 victory, and I had a feeling that things, all things, were starting to come together.